MW00478519

BLACK WORKS

- a novel –

By Eric Luthi

Copyright ©

by
Eric Luthi
2019

ISBN: 978-1-951721-01-5

Underwood Press LLC
Phoenix, Arizona
underwoodpressllc@gmail.com

For Emma, Roy, Margaret and Dalton,
and, of course, Ruth.

BLACK WORKS

ONE

"Teufel?" said the cowboy.

Gene Henry looked at him. He wore the right kind of hat and boots but he didn't look like he needed to shave or ever had.

"Teufel." Gene Henry nodded.

"What's that supposed to mean?"

"It means devil."

"Why not just name him Devil, then?"

"Guess the breeder thought it sounded meaner in German. Teufel. Kinda like the sound you make when you get gut punched."

"Sounds like 'toyful' to me."

"Yep. That, too."

"Like he's a toy?"

"More like we're the toys and he's gonna toss us around that ring."

"Really?" said the cowboy.

"He's a beast."

The cowboy thought about it for a moment. "I wonder who the rider is was unlucky enough to draw him."

Gene Henry looked at the bull.

"That would be me."

"Oh," said the cowboy.

Gene heard his name called and stepped up to the railing. He climbed onto the lowest rail and lifted himself up so the crowd could see him. The cheers erupted as soon as his head showed above the top rail.

"Gene Henry Comstock, ladies and gentlemen," said the announcer. "Two-time all-around champion defending his title this year."

Gene Henry took off his hat and waved once to the crowd. The crowd cheered again. He put his hat on the nearest post and put on his helmet and fastened the straps under his chin.

Teufel crashed into the railing and Gene Henry waited. When the bull calmed down, Gene lowered himself onto the bull's back as the handler held tight onto the rope. When he was set the handler passed the rope to the rider.

"You ready?" said the handler.

Gene looked at him and nodded.

"Ride 'em, cowboy," said the handler as he raised a thumb and leaned back from the railing.

The gate swung open and bull and rider flew out. The bull was crazy wild. Gene held as tight as he could, but only for a few seconds. The fourth buck threw him from the back of the bull. He tried to land on his feet but fell and tumbled away. The rodeo clowns moved in and so did the bull.

Teufel landed his hooves twice on the pesky rider that had been on his back. When the clowns and the wranglers drew the bull away Gene Henry lay still on the ground.

TWO

Hal watched the horses run in the field next to the dirt road. He took off his hat and wiped his brow. Looking first one way and then the other, he put his hat back on his head, shifted his rucksack and walked on. He heard the engine and turned before he saw the truck come over the rise. He watched but didn't raise a thumb. The dark blue Ford roared past without slowing down. Hal closed his eyes against the dust cloud that followed the car and let his breath out while he waited for it to pass.

Hal slapped the dust off his hat and then used the hat to dust off the rest of himself. Finished, he put the hat back on his head and walked on.

A quarter of an hour later, another car approached on the dirt road traveling in the same direction as the earlier truck. He stepped to the side of the road and watched the car approach.

Inside the car, an Oldsmobile Omega, the driver held a phone to his ear with one hand and steered with the other. Ahead, he saw Hal and took his foot off the gas pedal.

"I'll be a few minutes late," he said into the phone. "And I'll be bringing a guest." He stopped the car next to Hal and rolled down the window. The dust cloud that followed the car now flowed past them. The driver didn't roll up the window and some of the dust settled on the inside.

"Happy Fourth," said the driver.

"Same to you, mister."

"You going anywhere?"

Hal looked down the road, "That way."

"Any place in particular?"

"No place I can put a name to."

"I'm going to a Fourth of July picnic. Wanna come?"

Hal looked up the road and then the other direction and then back at the driver. "What makes you ask?"

"You look like a guy could use some food and some fireworks."

"That obvious, huh?"

"Well…"

Hal felt the sun on his neck and then stuck his hand through the open window. "Hal Comstock."

"Jim Rhodes."

Hal opened the door and slid into the passenger seat.

"Good to meet you, Jim."

"Same here. Hope you're hungry."

"I can always eat."

"I'm like that, too. Well, there'll be plenty

of food. My wife makes the best apple pie in the county."

Hal nodded. Jim put the car in gear and stepped on the gas, leaving the drifting cloud of dust behind.

"Hot day for a walk."

"Not too bad once you're used to it."

"Walk much?"

"Don't have a horse, don't have a car."

They drove for a moment in silence.

"Fourth of July picnic?"

"Church puts it on every year."

Hal noticed an ID tag hanging from the center console. A church ID, it held Jim's picture as well as the words, "Senior Pastor."

"No offense, pastor, but maybe you'd best let me out here."

"Aren't you hungry?"

"I'm always hungry."

"You got something against the Fourth of July?"

"I love the Fourth of July."

"You got something against pastors?"

"We don't always get along."

"Why is that?"

"I usually do or say something stupid."

"I wouldn't worry about it. My wife tells me I say stupid things all the time."

"Yeah, well..."

"Look, this is just a picnic. Good food and mostly good company. No preaching. If you don't like it, you don't have to stay. No obligation."

"Okay, but don't say I didn't warn ya."

Jim's wife, Nell, smiled and greeted guests she walked between the picnic tables. She spotted Gus and Abby and headed toward them. They spotted her as well and changed direction to meet her.

"Where's that husband of yours? We're almost ready to eat," said Gus.

"He's a few minutes out. He's bringing a guest."

"Uh, oh," Abby smiled.

Nell smiled back and raised one eyebrow.

"Ol' Jim's picked himself up another stray," said Gus.

"Mind yourself, Gus," said Abby.

"God bless him, but he can't save everyone."

Abby and Nell exchange a look.

"Here they come now," said Nell.

The Oldsmobile drove up the road toward the gate which, in simple lettering, said "Gustafson's."

Inside the car, Hal read the lettering. "I've heard of this ranch."

"Not surprising. Gus is known for his quarter horses."

"And bulls."

"And bulls."

Jim stopped the car and he and Hal got out.

"Lot of people for a church picnic," said Hal.

"A Fourth of July picnic. It's just that lots

of people around here go to church, too. Not all of them come to mine. But here are three of them that do."

Gus, Abby and Nell walked up to them.

"Jim, we've been holding lunch for you."

"Sorry 'bout that, Gus. Abby, Nell, this here's my friend, Hal. Hal, Gus Gustafson, his wife, Abby and this here is my Nell."

They shook hands all around.

"Any friend of Jim's is a friend of mine," said Gus.

"You're welcome here, Hal," said Abby.

"Hal, make yourself to home. Fill yourself a plate, over there. I've got some chores. I'll catch up with you in a bit," said Jim. He and Gus and the ladies walked toward the main tables. Hal headed for the food, filled a plate, grabbed a bottle of water and found an empty spot at a picnic table decked out with a red and white checkered tablecloth.

A little girl sat down at the table across from Hal. She had a scoop of coleslaw and an ear of corn on her plate next to a hot dog. She looked up at Hal.

"What's your name?" she said.

"Hal, what's yours?"

"Sarah."

Someone spoke at the far end of the tables. Hal paid no mind. He picked up the ear of corn, dripping with butter. Sarah watched him. She looked at the ear of corn and then put her palms together, fingertips pointed up. Hal put down the ear of corn and put his hands together as well. The crowd fell silent as Jim spoke.

"Lord, thank you for this day that you have given us, for the freedom to worship you, for good friends, old and new, and for the great meal that you have planned for us. We pray in your name, amen."

"Amen," sounded through the crowd and then the noise picked up again as the people began to eat and talk.

As Hal cleared his plate and threw the rest into the trash bin, Gus came up to him and slapped him on the shoulder.

"Hal, let me buy you a beer."

"Okay...beer? At a church picnic?"

"Ah, it's a Fourth of July picnic, really. And what's the Fourth of July without an ice cold?"

They walked past the tables where a young man in a cowboy hat talked to a group of younger kids. Hal and Gus stopped to watch. The young man spread his feet wide apart and bent his knees, back straight as if sitting on the back of an animal. His left hand down, he settled in. He lifted his right hand into the air and held up a thumb.

"Now you say it," he nodded toward the children.

"Ride 'em, cowboy," they screamed.

He turned his heels in and spurred the make-believe animal and then hopped around, keeping his legs spread and arching his back first forward and then whipping it backwards. His left hand stayed down around his belt and his right hand waved forward and backward and in circles in the air above his head.

"Yee haw."

The children screamed and laughed and clapped their hands.

"Count," the young man called out. "You count."

The children shouted, "One, two, three, four, five, six, seven, eight." At eight, the young man threw himself to the ground where he rolled once in the grass and then jumped back to his feet. He threw his fists into the air above his head. The children cheered. At that, he took a bow.

"He's a tough one."

"Again, do it again."

"Maybe later. These bulls really take it out on a fella."

Gus waved him over.

"Hal, I want you to meet my son, Dean. Dean this is Hal. Hal, I don't know your last name."

"Comstock," said Hal as he reached for Dean's hand.

"Like the mine?"

"Yeah."

"Good to meet you, Hal."

"Likewise. I liked your performance."

"That? That's just play for the kids."

"Looked real enough to me."

"You ride?" said Gus.

"Nah, not really."

"But you tried it?" said Dean.

"I guess everybody around here's tried it."

"Not everyone," said Gus.

"I'd better run, I still got chores from Mom," said Dean. "Pleased to meet you, Hal."

Dean walked off and Hal turned to Gus, "Where can I get that beer?"

The two walked around the big red barn. Hal took a moment to admire the horses in the corral. One horse stood separate from the others in an adjacent corral.

"Those are fine horses," said Hal.

"Yes, they are. That one," said Gus, pointing to the separate one, "is giving my boys a time, though."

"Why's that?"

"He's wild. Feisty. Just came in from a roundup. Doesn't want to take to the saddle. Thinking about saving him for the rodeo circuit."

"I didn't know there were that many wild ones still out there."

"They're there all right. Every once in a while the government likes to reduce the numbers so we get a chance to pick up one or two."

They reached the rear of the barn where another picnic table stood with a half oak barrel sitting next to it. The barrel held ice and water and cans and bottles of beer. Gus reached in and grabbed one and held it out for Hal.

"You got a specific brand?"

"Any port in a storm."

Hal took the beer and twisted off the cap.

"Amen to that," said Gus. He held out his own bottle and Hal touched it with his.

"Here's to it."

They each took a long swig and then sat down at the picnic table.

"So you tried bull riding? What about horses? Can you ride?"

"Even little kids can ride horses."

"Even so, some people are better at it."

They sat for a few moments watching the horses move around in the corral.

"Hal, let me ask you a question."

Hal tilted his head a bit and waited.

"Why are you here?"

"Jim invited me."

"Oh, I know that. But I wonder why you're here? You looking for work? You looking for a handout? What brings you 'round?"

"Just passing through. I'd take work if it's available."

"Hmm. Let me try it a little different. Where are you headed?"

"Jim asked me that, too."

"And what did you tell him?"

Hal points toward the road, "That way."

"It probably wouldn't come up any different if I asked you where you were coming from, would it?"

Hal tilted his head and rolled his eyes to look in the other direction with a hint of a smile on his lips.

Gus laughed. "That's what I thought." He paused for a breath. "Jim's a good man. We like him around here."

"I get that."

A man came around the barn, saw them and headed over.

"Boss, Abby's looking for you."

"Thanks, Charlie. Hal, help yourself to whatever you like and we'll catch up a bit more later on."

Hal raised his beer bottle and watched Gus disappear around the house. Two beers later, he looked at the main house. One more beer and he got up from the table.

He dropped the last bottle into the trash can and found his way into the house. Nobody moved around much inside beyond one or two people in the kitchen. No one said anything to Hal. He found a living room. He opened cabinets and found the liquor. Taking out a bottle and a glass, he unscrewed the top and poured himself half a glass of bourbon. He watched the glass for a moment and then filled it the rest of the way.

"Do you know anything about him?" Gus asked.

"A little bit," Jim answered.

"Do you want to fill me in? So we both know." Gus looked at Jim as Jim looked back over his shoulder at the people moving toward the house. They both stopped and turned to look back. Everyone seemed to be heading toward the corrals behind the barn.

"What in...?"

A noise near the house turned into cheers. As they moved closer, Gus and Jim could see a rider on a horse over the heads of the crowd. The two broke into a run.

In the corral, Hal sat on the stallion's back without saddle or reins. He gripped the flanks of the horse with his feet and had one hand in the long mane. He let the other hand swing above his head. The horse shied and kicked and bucked but could not dislodge its rider.

"One," Hal shouted as the hooves hit the ground after the first real buck and already a full two seconds into his ride and this only then after the horse had made a mad dash across the corral.

"Two," he grunted out the second number as the horse jarred him good as it landed all four hooves at the same instant.

"Three," the crowd took up the count as the hooves pounded into the dirt and sent dust and flecks of spittle flying. The horse's eyes were crazy with fear as much at the shouting from the crowd as from the rider on his back.

"Four." The horse lurched to the right and Hal slid toward the left and almost lost his seat on the horse.

"Five." The horse moved the opposite direction but Hal used the moment to grip the animal tighter with his knees and heels. His left hand still held onto the bunch of mane. Along with the horse, his own spit now flew out of his mouth as each impact forced his breath out between clenched teeth.

Together now with the crowd, Hal kept counting.

"Six."

The horse reared and threw its head back and hit Hal in the face. Blood dripped from his nose and spattered onto his shirt. The horse bucked harder to try to dislodge its rider.

"Seven."

The crowd screamed the count now but Hal no longer heard them. He heard only the horse breathing hard and saw it trying to look back at him.

"Eight."

Eight times the horse flung itself into the air, four feet off the ground and arched its back. Eight times Hal hung on through the bone-jarring crunch as the hooves hit the ground and his butt slammed into the animal's back. Eight times by his count and the people screaming the numbers. Eight full seconds and more.

On the ninth landing, Hal swung his leg across the horse's back and let go of the mane. He landed on his feet and jumped backward. The horse, now free, skittered across to the far side of the corral and stayed there.

Hal didn't hear the cheers and barely felt the hands that grabbed him as he fell to his knees at fence.

The hands pulled Hal through the rails of the corral and laid him in the dirt.

"Is he hurt?"

"He's bleeding."

"Give him room."

Gus and Jim came up. Charlie knelt next to Hal and leaned in close and then drew back and waved his hand under his own nose. "I don't think he's hurt. But he is drunk."

Several in the crowd laughed.

Charlie shook Hal's shoulder but Hal didn't move. "Hey bud, time to get up."

Still no answer.

"Yeah," said Gus. He stood up straight and looked at the horse still in the corral. "Charlie, go check out the horse. Give him some water and see if he'll let you brush him down." Then he looked over to Jim. "He can sleep it off here. You can leave him to me. I'll send him on his way when he sobers up."

"No, I brought him," said Jim. "I'll take him with me."

"Sure?"

"Yeah. Help me get him into the car."

THREE

It was the quiet that startled Hal. Then, the sunlight. Then, the bed.

He looked down at his feet. Socks and no boots. He still wore his jeans but his shirt wasn't tucked in and his belt lay on the side table. Hal sat up and groaned with the effort. He rubbed the back of his head and then felt the rest to see what part hurt most.

He sat on the edge of the bed for a few moments and took a few deep breaths. The small room held a single bed with a picture of an angel escorting two little kids across a bridge on one wall and a picture of John Wayne sitting on a horse on the other wall.

Hal found his boots at the foot of the bed and pulled them on. Next, his belt. He left his shirt untucked and found his rucksack. The door opened on to a stairway. He tried to go down the wooden stairs without noise but his boots wouldn't let him. The stairway ended with another door. He opened it into the sunlight and squinted at the bright light. He had been in a room over the barn.

A house stood across the dirt yard and next to it a driveway which led to the road. He headed for that.

A door on the porch opened and Nell stood there looking at him. Hal stopped but didn't say anything. Nell waited. Hal took his hat off. Nell pointed a finger at him, turned her palm upwards and then crooked her finger back.

Hal ducked his head and headed toward her. He stopped at the foot of the steps.

"Coffee?"

"Please."

"Sit yourself down." She backed away but left the door open. Hal wiped his boots on the mat and walked into the bright yellow kitchen. Nell got a cup from the rack by the sink and set it in front of Hal and filled it.

"How do you take it?"

"Black works."

Nell put the coffee pot back on counter and turned around to look at him. She leaned back against the counter and had her arms crossed. Hal swallowed a gulp and then put the cup down on the table.

"I did something stupid, didn't I?"

"That depends on who you ask."

"If you ask Gus, you did something real dumb," said Jim as he walked into the kitchen. "And he's pretty pissed. But that's Gus."

Nell handed Jim a mug and he poured himself a cup. He turned back to Hal.

"Look," said Hal. "I...uh...I'm..."

Jim waived him off and Hal stopped talking.

"You a cowboy?"

"Was. Maybe still am."

"When's the last time you set a horse?"

"Been a while."

"Before yesterday, I mean."

"I rode a horse?"

Jim and Nell looked at each other.

"If you call that riding," said Nell.

"Did I fall off?"

Jim coughed but managed to keep the coffee in his mouth. Nell turned to the sink. Hal looked down at his cup.

"If you call that falling," Jim said after he cleared his throat.

Hal swirled the coffee left in his cup.

"Got any tack?" said Jim.

"Drank it all."

Jim went to the window and looked out, waiting. "This is my ranch. It's not nearly as big as Gus'. I do most of it myself. I could use some help. You interested?"

Hal shook his head. "Are you offering me a job?"

"Doesn't pay much and the work's hard."

"I drink too much, sometimes."

"Nell tells me I preach too much, sometimes."

"You ever preach so much you passed out?"

"No. Not yet."

"Well, then."

"Well, then," said Jim. "Ain't a one of us perfect."

Hal didn't answer.

"You can sleep in the room you're in," said Nell. "It's our son's. He preferred it out there to the main house. He stayed at school this summer."

"Are you offering me work because you need help or because you think I need it?"

"Does it matter?" said Jim.

"Maybe."

"Like I said, I could use some help. And when I can't use you, my neighbor Jenet can. She's got a ranch a little bigger than mine and no regular help. Her husband's gone and her son's not interested in ranching. I'm pretty sure I can speak for her."

"Okay."

Jim and Nell look at each other.

"You got to understand, Hal. This is a dry ranch. That means there's no alcohol on it and there won't be."

"Okay."

"Okay," said Jim.

"Oh-kay," said Nell. "Jim, you take Hal out and show him around. Hal, you'll take meals with us and lunch is in an hour."

"Yes, ma'am."

Outside, Jim and Hal walked around the

house and barn and the attached corral.

"Nothing special. Cattle mostly and a few horses."

"Cattle and horses?"

"Don't seem right really, one without the other."

"Like ranching and preaching?"

Jim laughed. "Sort of."

Out in the field, a horse and rider approached. The rider, a girl on a brown mare, waved as she got closer. Hal recognized Sarah, the girl from the picnic.

"She yours?" asked Hal while she was still out of earshot.

"She is."

Jim opened the gate to the corral and Sarah walked her horse in. Jim closed the gate behind her as Sarah threw one leg over the horse and slid off.

"Hi, dad. Hi mister Hal."

"Hi, Sarah," said Hal.

"Are you staying?" asked Sarah.

"It seems so."

"Oh, good. I was hoping you'd say yes."

Hal looked over to Jim whose mouth edged up in a smile.

"For a while, at least," said Hal.

"Sarah, put your horse away and get cleaned up. Lunch is almost ready."

Sarah walked the horse into the barn. They watched her go.

"Tomorrow morning, I'll let you muck out the barn. We strip them out complete every other Saturday, less often in the summer when the horses stay in the field more. I hope the smell don't bother you too much. Most people get used to it. Some never do, though."

"I don't mind the smell."

"No, I didn't think you would."

The screen door slammed behind Sarah as she disappeared into the kitchen.

"Let's go in. Nell will be up after us if we're late to the table."

FOUR

Hal got up before the sun and, after a cup of coffee from Nell's kitchen to fortify him, headed back to the barn. He pulled the barn doors open. Both doors squeaked but one complained louder than the other. Inside the doors to the right sat a large workbench littered with tools, two tool-boxes, various riding and livestock tack, and the odd piece of straw. Hal poked around until he found an oil can that had oil in it. He applied the oil to all the hinges on the doors and opened and closed the doors to work the oil in. When the squeaking stopped, he returned the oil can to the bench.

The wall behind the workbench held some pegs and there were additional pegs on some of the posts throughout. He sorted through the tools and equipment on the bench. He hung the halters and bits and bridles on the pegs. The leathers needed oiling.

The tools he sorted into the two tool-boxes. Some, like the saws, were too big to fit. These he hung on the wall above the bench.

He found a pitchfork and long-handled

shovel and a wheelbarrow that had seen a lot of use. He loaded the pitchfork and the shovel into the wheelbarrow and rolled it over to the first stall. All of the horses were already outside in the field.

With the pitchfork, Hal piled the manure and old straw as high as he could into the wheelbarrow. The muck pile sat fifty yards beyond the corral behind the barn. It was far enough away to discourage the flies from getting to the horses and still downwind from the house. After his third trip, he came back to find Sarah sitting on the top rail of the stall next in line for cleaning.

"Hi, Mister Hal."

"Hal is good."

"Hi, Mister Hal is good."

"And how are you, Sarah?"

"Sarah is good, too."

"And speaking of herself in third person."

"Huh?"

"That's what it means when you talk about yourself like you were someone else or somewhere else."

Sarah looked confused.

"Without saying 'I' or 'me,'" Hal said.

"Oh."

Hal forked a load into the wheelbarrow.

"They say Napoleon did that," Hal said as he pitched another.

"Spoke about himself like he wasn't there?"

"Yes."

"Oh." She paused for a second. "I thought you were a cowboy."

"Well, maybe."

"But you talk like an English teacher."

"I just paid attention in school."

"Oh."

With the wheelbarrow full and the stall almost empty, Hal leaned the pitchfork against the wall and picked up the shovel and scrapped the floor for what remained.

"Can you teach me to ride like that?"

"Like what?"

"Like you rode up at mister Gustafson's ranch."

Hal stopped working and looked up at Sarah. Then he scraped the floor some more and scooped the muck into the wheelbarrow.

"I don't remember all that much after lunch that day."

"Really?"

"I remember the corn. It was good."

"It was."

Hal took hold of the handles of the wheelbarrow, lifted and walked toward the door. Sarah jumped down and followed him.

"You rode that wild horse like he was tame. All the people watched and yelled and counted."

"They counted?"

"You were counting first."

"I was counting?"

"You were. All the way up to eight."

"Well, I don't know what I was thinking."

Sarah stopped and stared at him as Hal kept on to the muck pile.

"You don't?"

"If I was thinking, I sure don't remember."

She broke into a run to catch up to him.

"Papa says people who drink too much don't always remember what happens to them or what they do."

"Yeah, I'm one of those."

"My grandpa was, too."

"Was what?"

"One of those who drank too much and couldn't remember."

Hal looked at her, "I'm sorry."

"I never met him. My Momma told me."

"Still..."

"So, can you teach me?"

"I saw you ride. You already ride well."

"I'd ride better if you teach me."

Hal rolled the wheelbarrow to the pile and dumped it. He used the shovel to clean up the edge and throw the debris higher up onto the pile.

"I can teach you some rope tricks if you like. As for the riding, you're going to have to ask your Pop if he'll let me teach you."

"He'll say yes."

"If he does, then I'll teach you."

"Thank you mister Hal is good."

"Remember, your dad has to say so."

"I know."

"And your Momma."

"Okay."

Sarah ran off toward the house. Hal turned the wheelbarrow back to the barn. Sarah stopped running and turned around, still walking backward to the house.

"I know what you were doing at mister Gustafson's ranch." She still walked backwards so she could see Hal while she spoke.

Hal stopped to look back at her. "Oh? What was that?"

"You were pretending you were in a rodeo."

Hal watched her as she turned and ran the rest of the way back to the house.

FIVE

"Sarah says you want to teach her to ride," Jim said as he passed the mashed potatoes to Hal. Hal looked first at Sarah then at Jim and then scooped a serving onto his plate.

"Sarah asked me if I would teach her."

"And you said?"

"I said she had to ask you."

"And me," said Nell.

"And you," said Jim. "Hal, what do you think?"

Hal chewed the food in his mouth and swallowed it.

"I think she already rides well."

"Sarah?" Jim looked to his daughter.

"Yes, Daddy?"

"What is it you want Mr. Hal to teach you?"

"I want to ride like he does."

"You only saw him ride once."

"Yes, but he looked like he was riding rodeo."

"And you want to ride in a rodeo?"

"I want to ride a bronco."

"There are other events in rodeo besides

bucking," said Nell. "Barrel riding and roping would work."

"I would do those. But I also want to learn to ride a bronco. Other girls do."

"I don't really ride like that anymore," said Hal.

"You rode like that at Gus's place," said Nell.

"I was falling down drunk at Gus's place."

"You rode like that when you were falling down drunk," said Sarah.

"Sarah," said Jim.

"Sorry."

No one spoke for a few moments.

"I rode like that because I was falling down drunk. I wouldn't have gotten on that horse if I were sober."

Again silence at the table.

"Are you willing to teach her?"

"Barrel riding and roping?" said Hal.

"And bronco?" said Sarah.

"Barrel riding and roping first," said Jim.

"I'll teach her what I can."

Jim looked at Hal, then at Sarah and last at Nell.

"Nell?"

"No bulls?"

"No bulls."

"If she wants to learn, let her learn."

SIX

Gus stood alone by the railing of the corral. Inside, Charlie and another hand held tight onto the black's reins while Dean struggled to mount the saddle. The horse shied and pulled back.

"Don't let him scare you, Dean," Gus shouted. "Get on 'im."

Dean got his left foot into the stirrup and that's as far as he got. The horse reared up and pulled the reins away from the handlers. Dean fell back and the horse scampered off to the far side of the corral.

"Still giving you a time?" said Jim at Gus' elbow.

Gus turned his head. "Didn't see you come up, Jim. You practicing your ninja moves, now?"

"Nah, my ninja moves will stay right as they are. I got too many other things to practice first."

Gus reached over and shook Jim's hand.

"What brings you by?"

"Just wanted to see how you're doing."

"Well, as you can see."

Inside the corral, Dean and Charlie were

trying to herd the horse into a spot where they could grab the reins. The horse wanted otherwise and evaded them or pulled free time and again.

"Dean still trying to break him?"

"Dean is."

"No luck?"

"Nobody rides him for long, if at all."

"Why could Hal ride him?"

"I don't know about that. Your boy was drunk. Maybe he slipped him some of those beers he was drinking or even something stronger. Maybe doped him up with some of that bourbon he found."

"Nah, you think so?"

"All I know is he did something. Otherwise, no way he would have stayed on that horse. And, whatever he did, no one rides him now. Which makes him useless to me on the ranch. I'm still thinking of putting him on the rodeo circuit. Let those cowboys deal with him."

In the kitchen, Nell picked up the phone on the first ring.

"Hello."

She listened for a few seconds.

"See you in a few."

Nell hung up the phone and turned to Sarah who shelled peas at the table.

"You'd better finish those up quick."

"Why, Momma?"

Jim's Oldsmobile pulled up the long driveway and parked by the house. Hal had just finished watering and feeding the horses and headed over to where Jim stood when he saw Gus's truck coming up the driveway pulling a trailer. The driver, Charlie, stopped the truck by the two men. Jim pointed toward the corral and Charlie eased the truck in that direction.

Jim looked at Hal. Hal raised an eyebrow. Jim walked to the corral and Hal followed him.

A scream sounded from inside the house. It stopped Hal, but Jim kept walking. Hal looked to the house, then to Jim, and then back to the house as another scream sounded. The door burst open and Sarah bounced out and ran past them to where the trailer was now parked by the corral.

Nell followed her out the kitchen door at a slower pace.

Sarah jumped on to the trailer's fender and grabbed at the bars to look in.

"Careful," said Jim. "He's far from a tame horse."

"Oh, Daddy. He's beautiful. Does he have a name?"

Nell came up to the trailer and looked in. Hal stepped up as well.

"He came in from the wild and Gus never gave him a name," said Charlie. He undid the bolts holding the gate shut. Hal reached through the window and untied the horse. He clicked his tongue and backed the horse out of the trailer. Once out, Hal walked the horse to the corral and removed the halter. The horse galloped away across the corral and Hal closed the gate. Sarah climbed on the gate a second later.

"I guess that will be your first chore," said Jim. "Naming him."

"I can pick his name?"

"Don't see why not."

"The boys were thinking 'Midnight,'" said Charlie.

"A lot of black horses are called 'Midnight," said Hal, still watching from the gate.

"Blackie?" said Sarah.

Nell laughed. "Now he sounds like a kitten."

"How 'bout we just call him 'Ralph'?" said Jim. Everyone stared at him. "Okay, never mind."

Nell looked over at Hal. "How did you say you liked your coffee, Hal?"

"Uh, black."

"No you didn't. You said 'black works.'"

Jim looked from Nell to Hal. "Black works? Black works. Black Works. That fits just fine."

"You know it'll just get shortened to Black?" said Hal.

"Yeah, around here I'm sure. Or even Blackie," Jim said as he looked at Sarah. "But in competitions, in the lists, it'll show up as Black Works. And that's a good name for a competitor."

"Black Works," nodded Charlie.

"Black," said Nell.

"Blackie," said Sarah.

SEVEN

Sarah came out of the kitchen door on Saturday morning and headed straight over to the barn. She found Hal brushing down the black horse.

"Good morning, mister Hal."

"Really, Hal is fine."

"Okay. What will you teach me, today?"

"I'm thinking we work on roping."

"Roping?"

"Yes."

"Can I ride Blackie?"

"I don't think that's a good idea, yet."

"Why not?"

"'Cause he's big and mean and scary," said Hal as he held his fingers next to his face as if he had claws.

"Nah."

"No, not really. But he is wild and you have other things to learn first. Besides, I found a small sore on his back.

"Is he hurt?"

"Not much but it looks fairly new. Look here," he said as he separated the hair on the horse's back and showed her the raw wound. "Here, you do it."

Sarah put her fingers around the wound to hold the hair away from the blood.

Hal pulled a small pair of scissors out of his shirt pocket and trimmed the hair all around the bloody patch. "The hair dries into the scab and when he runs or turns, the hair pulls the scab apart and it bleeds again. And it must hurt a bit."

When he finished the trimming, Hal stepped over to the workbench and brought back a small tube. He unscrewed the cap and handed it to Sarah.

"What's this?"

"Ointment. Antibiotic. I got it from your Mom. It'll keep the scab soft for a while and help it heal quicker. Especially now that the hair's trimmed back."

"How did he get this?"

"Who knows? The saddle may have had a rough spot and rubbed him wrong or something got under it."

Sarah went to the horse and stroked his forehead and face. "Poor Blackie."

"Anyhow, I think we should let that heal before anyone tries to ride him again, okay?"

"Okay."

Hal came out of the stall and went over to the equipment rack. He took down a coiled length of rope and handed it to Sarah. She uncoiled part of it and inspected the knot and rubbed the rope between her fingers.

"Is this a lasso?"

"It's a rope."

"No, this is one of those lariat thingys?"

"It's a rope."

"Is it really just a rope?"

"It's not a lariat and it's not a lasso and really, really not a thingy. To a cowboy -- and a cowgirl -- this is a rope."

Sarah sighed as she rolled her eyes up and to the side. "Okay."

"Now, you ever use a rope?"

"Sure, lots of times."

"Not a jump rope."

"No, not really. Only a little."

"That's okay. That's why you're here. Now, untie that knot."

Sarah worked at it for a few minutes. The tight knot and stiff rope made her struggle.

"It's a lot harder to untie a knot than it is to tie it in the first place. Keep going."

Sarah worked the knot until it loosened. She looked up at Hal.

"Watch how it comes apart so you can tie it again."

He watched her untie the knot. She held the rope up to show him.

"Good. The rope we use is stiffer than say a nylon rope you might use around the house. This rope has been tied in that knot for a while so the bends still show and the fibers are compressed where the knot pressed against them. See?"

"Yes."

"Good. Now tie the knot back."

She crossed the rope over itself being careful to match up the bends in the rope. Finally, she pulled the end of the rope through the last hole and pulled the knot tight.

"Very good. That's called a hondo."

"The knot?"

"Yes."

"Won't the end slip through?"

"Most cowboys use a natural fiber rope like this one. The rope has a lot of friction and the fibers kind of grab onto each other. A rope like this won't slide as easy as a nylon rope will. But if you're worried about it, you can always tie a stopper knot. That'll put an end to any chance at it slipping."

"Why not just use a bowline?"

"A bowline?"

"Yeah. A bowline won't slip and you don't need the stopper knot."

"Where did you learn about bowlines?"

"I was a Brownie. Mom taught me. She was the Owl for our troop."

"Brownies learn to tie knots?"

"We did."

Hal looked at Sarah while he thought about it.

"Bowlines are for boats. Hondos are for horse work. But you can use any knot that works for you. No one will ever know and, if anyone does look, you don't get judged on your knots. You want to be able to pinch the knot so the noose stays open when you throw it over the calf's head. And you want to be able to pull the noose closed once you've done that. So try 'em both and see which one you like better when you're throwing. I'll ask you later to show me both."

"Okay."

"Good. Now, go practice your knots."

Sara spooned up cereal from a bowl at the table. Nell sat across from her and watched her eat.

"Momma?"

"Yes?"

"Why are you staring at me?"

"Can't a mother look at her daughter?"

"Yes, Momma."

Nell watched her as she held her spoon with her fingertips. She had always gripped it before using her whole hand. Nell reached across the table and took Sarah's hand and turned it over. Sarah's palm was red and chaffed. Nell took Sarah's other hand and inspected it. More of the same. Sarah looked up at her mother.

"Hal says my hands will toughen up as I handle the ropes more."

Nell nodded. "You make sure you wash your hands and put some lotion on every time after you handle the rope."

"Yes, Momma."

"I can wax the rope to keep the loose fibers down," said Hal.

"Is that legal?" said Nell.

"Nothing in the rules about it that I know of."

"Won't that make it harder to keep the noose open?" said Jim.

"We just won't wax that part of the rope or the knot. But we can wax everywhere else until her hands develop some calluses."

"I don't know that I want her to have calluses."

"I've never met a true cowgirl who had smooth hands."

"And she's probably already got calluses that you don't know about."

"Great. Now she'll have hands like her father."

EIGHT

Sarah's chores included feeding and brushing Blackie. The horse was getting used to her and she thought he acted glad to see her every time she came into the stable. He would come over to her and nuzzle her. She still treated his sore with the ointment every day, although it was harder to spot, now.

Sarah fished into her pocket and pulled out at carrot and held it out for Blackie. He made a whinnying sound as he took the carrot into his mouth.

"When can I ride him?" she asked Hal.

"Soon."

"How soon?"

"He's almost ready. The sore is healed up. I just want to make sure you two are friends."

"We're friends, aren't we Blackie."

"A few more days, then."

"Will he try to throw me?"

"I don't think so. Maybe."

Sarah stood ten feet from a post driven into the ground. She coiled the rope in her left hand as she eyed the post. She spun the noose end over her head a couple of times and then launched it at the post. She missed and coiled the rope again for another try.

A blue pickup truck pulled up to the house. Sarah stopped to watch. Dean got out and waved to her. She waved back as he walked over to her.

"How's it coming?"

"Watch me."

Sarah swung the rope over her head twice and then threw it at the post. The noose slipped down over the post and she pulled it tight. Dean clapped his hands.

"Wonderful. That's great."

"I make it about half the time."

"Still like it?"

"Yes. Hal says we're going to do a moving target next and then after that I'll be on a horse and then a moving target from a moving horse."

"And when you're roping calves, you'll be big time. "

"Well, maybe."

"I know you will. Is Hal around?"

"He's working fences today."

"Oh."

"He's been gone for a few hours. Should be back for lunch."

Nell came out of the kitchen door. "Dean."

"Hello, Mrs. Rhodes."

"Would you and Sarah like some Lemonade?"

Sarah finished her lemonade first.

"May I be excused? I have to go practice."

"Of course. Put your glass in the sink."

Nell and Dean watched as Sarah went out to the post and took up the rope hanging on it. They had a clear view through the kitchen window.

"She's doing well."

"She does enjoy it."

"And you?"

"She's young."

"My pop says you were a barrel racer once."

"Yeah and I tried roping, too. But not broncs. Too wild, too crazy. I do seem to remember that your Pop was a bull rider once."

"And now he's a clown."

"Bullfighter."

"Bullfighter."

They sat for a moment watching Sarah.

"Why did you give it up?"

"I got busy with other things. Went to college. Met Jim."

Sarah roped the post for the third time in a row.

"There are lady riders, bulls even."

"Not many."

"They say the lighter riders do better."

"Dean, she's only ten."

"She's just started roping. There's a long way to go before she's onto broncs. She may change her mind."

"I hope so."

They see a rider approaching along the

fence line.

"Hal's back."

"I didn't think he was riding."

"We don't have an ATV. Besides, Hal says he likes to do it on horseback instead of on a motor."

Dean met Hal at the stable.

"Dean, what brings you out?"

"Just stopped by. Actually, I wanted to see you."

Dean took the saddlebags off the horse while Hal undid the saddle. He lifted it off and set it on the bench. Dean removed the bridle and Hal pulled the blanket off the horse's back. He took a brush and handed a second one to Dean. Each brushed his side of the horse. They worked for a few minutes before Dean spoke.

"I tried to ride the stallion before Jim bought him."

Hal nodded.

"I tried several times and was never able to stay on or to control him for more than a few seconds."

"He had a sore. I'm sure it irritated him."

"But you rode him."

"Bareback. I'm sure you used a saddle."

"I did."

"That may be all it was."

"You think so?"

"I don't know. Probably."

"But you were drunk when you rode him."

"Yeah."

"Not that – I mean – you were drunk and you still rode him. Really well. Really well despite being drunk. I don't know anyone who could do that."

"How many drunks do you know?"

"Oh, I know a few."

"Well, I don't remember the ride at all. I can't tell you what I did or why I did it. I remember drinking some beers and then waking up the next morning here."

"You were great. You looked good out there. I wish someone had filmed it so I could prove it to you."

Hal stopped brushing, "I was drunk."

"Yeah. I know."

"I don't need any film of that."

They both brushed again.

"That's not the reason I came to see you." When Hal didn't answer, Dean went on, "I want to know if you'll teach me some about riding."

"You already ride well and you break horses. What can I teach you?"

"I'm not here about horses."

Hal kept brushing.

"I can ride horses as well as the next guy. Not as good as you, but good enough."

Hal stopped brushing the horse and came around to Dean's side. He took the brush from Dean and put both brushes on their hooks on the wall. He turned back to Dean.

"Teach me how to ride a bull."

"Bulls?"

"You rode that horse like he was a toy. You said you'd ridden bulls before. From the way you rode that stallion -- you've ridden something bigger – something tougher. Teach me how to ride a bull."

"I don't ride bulls anymore."

"You don't have to ride. Just teach me."

Hal led the horse back to his stable and latched the gate behind it.

"Your father was a bull rider and he still raises bulls."

"Yeah."

"What did he teach you?"

"My dad is – well – he's my father."

Hal rested his foot on the lowest railing of the gate. "Jim doesn't have any bulls."

"I can get a bull."

"From your father?"

"Yes, but I'll bring him here."

"The bull or your father?"

"The bull. But my father probably won't stay away either."

"Well, you'll still have to ask your father and we'll both have to ask Jim and Nell, first."

"Got to keep him separated," Jim said at supper that night.

"He'll calm down if you keep some steers in with him."

"He won't attack them?"

"Probably not."

"You're not sure."

"Not a hundred percent."

"This is becoming quite the teaching job for you," said Nell. "First Sarah and now Dean. Perhaps you should advertise as a rodeo school."

"I'm not looking for a new job."

"I guess I'm okay with it," said Jim.

"What about me?" said Sarah.

"No bull riding," said Nell.

"Mom?"

"You heard your mother," said Jim.

"Okay."

The next morning Gus's truck pulled into the Rhodes' driveway once again. Charlie drove and Dean rode as passenger. The truck pulled the same livestock trailer that delivered Black Works a couple of weeks earlier.

Hal came out of the barn and met the truck.

"Brought you a loaner," said Charlie.

"Snodgrass," said Dean.

"What kind of name is that?"

"Gus named him after a teacher he said left a bad taste in his mouth."

"Ah. Good to see you Dean."

"Hal."

"Let's get him out of the trailer. Back it up to the gate there."

Dean jumped out and Charlie maneuvered

the end of the trailer back toward the gate. Dean opened the gate before the trailer got to it. The gate and the trailer filled up the opening so the animal would have no other way to go but into the corral.

Nell and Sarah came out of the house to watch. Nell stood behind Sarah and put her arms around Sarah's shoulders and linked one hand over the other wrist.

The corral already contained two steers brought in from a field. The bull in the trailer banged against the side and the steers snorted and stayed on the far end of the corral.

Nell and Sarah moved closer to the corral but stayed back from the fence and from the trailer.

Hal pulled the gate back and went to the end of the trailer and unlatched one side.

"Careful, Hal," said Sarah as Hal walked to the other side of the trailer where only one latch now held the rear door closed.

"He's head in," said Hal. "He has to back out first before he can turn so I'll have time to get out of the way."

"You want me to do anything?" said Dean.

"Just make sure that gate stays against the trailer nice and tight."

Charlie went to stand with Dean to lend a hand if needed. Hal threw the latch bolt open and the door fell to the ground and made a ramp. Hal jumped to the fence and climbed over as Snodgrass backed out, banging his horns on the sides a few of times to show the trailer who was boss.

When the bull's head cleared the door, he spotted Hal and moved away from him. The steers already in the corral turned to face the newcomer and moved a few steps toward the center of the corral. The bull spotted their movement and turned sideways to the steers.

Sarah and Nell moved up to stand next to Hal and watch the bull and the steers in the corral.

"They're sizing each other up," said Hal in a low voice.

One of the steers took another step toward the bull. The bull moved his head from side to side and the steers retreated.

"Now he's the boss."

"Are they friends now?" said Sarah.

"Maybe not yet, but they will be."

The bull now walked over to where the two steers waited. The steers nuzzled the bull and the three animals walked around each other and stayed together.

"All right, Charlie."

Charlie got into the truck and turned the key. He eased the truck forward and Dean closed and latched the gate once the trailer cleared the opening.

"Where'd you learn to do that?" said Nell.

"Do what?"

"Mix the steers and the bull."

Hal looked back at the bull and the steers

together in the corral and then smiled at Nell, "Hemingway."

"Hemingway? You read Hemingway?"

Hal smiled and ducked his head.

"What was that for?"

"I thought you were going to ask me if I knew how to read."

Nell laughed and made a fist and punched him on the arm. They stood for a moment and watched the bull and steers in the corral.

"Now what?" Nell said.

"Now we have a bull."

"A loaner."

"Yep. We'll feed 'em in a bit, but first Sarah's going to show us how she can rope a post."

"Do I have to?"

"You're going to have to in the competition so you might as well get used to having an audience."

NINE

Gus' wife, Abby, lay in bed at home reading a book when Gus came into the room. He joined her in the bed and she put her book down on the nightstand.

"So Dean's going to try bull riding again," she said.

"Yeah."

"And he asked Hal to teach him."

"Yeah."

"You okay with that?"

"Dean's growed up."

"That's not an answer to the question I asked."

"I'm okay with Dean looking elsewhere for help. I'm not so sure about Hal. I'm not sure I trust him."

Abby looked at Gus and waited.

"I don't like the way he showed up. I don't like it that he doesn't answer questions about himself. Something just doesn't set right."

"Gus, he's just a stray and looking to find himself."

"I shot the last stray showed up around

here."

Abby reached out and smacked Gus on the shoulder with the back of her hand. "Gus."

"I meant the dog. The one that attacked the calf."

"I know what you meant."

Abby turned and cuddled up to Gus.

"Dean's just trying to please you. The fact that he's still trying to ride bulls when he really wants to be on the ground should tell you that."

"He wants to be on the ground?"

"He wants to be a clown."

"Clown? Bullfighter?"

"Sorry, bullfighter. Yes. I always forget you guys changed what you call yourselves now."

"He wants to be a bullfighter?"

"He wants to be like his father."

"He never mentioned that to me."

"There's things a boy will tell his mother that he won't tell his father. Yes. And why don't they call it 'bullfighting school' instead of 'rodeo clown school?'"

Gus sighed.

TEN

Hal brought Black Works out into the horse corral. The horse had a bridle but no saddle. Nell, Jim, Sarah and Dean, who had come by for a visit, stood on the other side of the fence, watching. Sarah wore a helmet.

"You think this is a good idea?" said Nell.

"Sooner or later," said Jim. "Hal knows what he's doing."

Hal stroked the horse's forehead. "Okay, Sarah."

Nell hugged Sarah, "Good luck. You'll be great."

Sarah climbed over the fence and walked over to the horse. He whinnied as she moved next to him. Hal still held the reins.

"Ready?"

Sarah nodded. She put a foot into Hal's outstretched hand and he lifted as she put her other foot over the horse's back. Blackie shimmied to the right a bit. Hal stroked the horse's forehead again.

"Talk to him."

Sarah leaned forward and whispered into

Blackie's ear. Blackie threw his head back made a chirping sound.

"Why no saddle?" said Nell.

"I want him to get used to her first," said Hal. "He's been wearing the bridle for a while, now. He's used to the bit. Later we introduce the saddle. By then, he won't care."

Hal stepped to Blackie's head. "Okay, sit up straight now."

Sarah sat with her back straight.

Nell raised her cell phone and took a picture with it.

"I want you to hold his mane gently but you are holding on mostly with your feet and legs. It's okay to grip him with your shoes."

Hal took her foot and moved it slightly higher on Blackie's flank.

Sarah squeezed Blackie with her legs. She wore tennis shoes so as not to scare him. Hal walked backward and Blackie followed him as the reins pulled taut. Hal walked backward halfway around the corral and then he turned his back to the horse. Hal kept walking until he made a complete circuit around the corral.

"Still doing okay?"

"We're both doing good."

"Then let's speed things up." Hal broke into a jog. The horse still walked although a bit faster. Hal went twice more around the corral and then stopped in front of Nell and Jim. He handed the reins to Sarah.

"He's going to follow me one more lap and then I'm going to get out of the way."

"Okay."

Hal walked one more lap and then climbed out of the corral. Blackie watched him for a moment wondering what to do.

Hal clicked his tongue. The horse still didn't move. "Use your feet a bit."

Sarah nudged the horse with her heels. Blackie walked forward and kept going around the corral. Sarah and Blackie went around five more times before Hal climbed back over the fence. Hal took the reins from Sarah as they came up to him.

"I think that's enough for today. We want to make sure he wants you back."

Sarah patted Blackie's neck as she swung her leg over his back and slid to the ground. Hal caught her and raised his hand and Sarah turned around and high-fived him.

"Take him inside now."

Hal handed the reins back to Sarah and she led Blackie into the stable. Hal turned to Nell and Jim, "She did well."

"You are something with horses," said Jim.

Hal nodded and turned to Dean, "Your turn."

"Now?"

"Tomorrow morning. Bring your gear."

ELEVEN

A pale Dean showed up the next morning at Nell's kitchen door.

"Coffee?"

"No. Can't keep it down."

"Just as well. Hal and Jim are waiting for you."

Dean got his gear bag from his truck and went out to the barn. The bull and a steer were in one of the smaller pens and the single steer was penned by itself off to the side of the corral in a pen not much larger than the animal in it. The pen had a makeshift gate held shut with baling wire instead of a latch. He found Jim and Hal in the barn. Dean dropped his bag on the ground next to them.

"I'd say you look chipper but I'd be lying," said Hal.

"I'm okay."

"Really?"

"No." Dean got the word out before he rushed for a corner where he threw up into the straw. Jim and Hal looked at one another.

"Sorry," said Dean as he returned to them wiping his mouth on his sleeve.

Hal handed him a bottle of water. "Wash and spit first. Then drink."

Dean spat out the first mouthful and then spat out two more before swallowing a small amount to wet his throat.

"Is this a normal event?" said Hal.

Dean nodded.

"I knew a professional bull rider, once. A champion. He threw up before every single competition ride. Every one. Even after he won the all-around, twice."

"Really?"

"Yep. It's no big deal. Show me your equipment."

Dean pulled out the equipment and handed it, one piece at a time, to Hal for inspection. Hal examined the gloves, the chaps, the rope, the spurs and the protective vest. After seeing all of it, Hal said, "Where's your helmet?"

"I wear a hat."

"Why not a helmet?"

"I've heard it affects your balance."

"And makes you look like a sissy?"

"Yeah," Dean laughed. "That, too."

"That's what the old timers say," said Hal. He looked to Jim, "The real cowboys."

"Yeah?"

"The ones who get their brains knocked loose and never ride again. The ones who can't stop their hands from shaking."

Dean said nothing.

"I'm not one of those guys," said Hal.

"My father says..."

Hal held up his hand and Dean stopped. "If you want your father to teach you, go ask him. You can ride and wear nothing but a Speedo if you want."

Jim squeezed his eyes shut, "Oh."

"Here -- with me -- you will wear a helmet every time you ride."

"I don't have a helmet."

Jim went to the workbench and came back carrying Sarah's helmet. "Just so happens I have one here." He handed the helmet to Dean who tried it on.

"It's too small."

"Exhale," said Hal.

"What?"

Jim smiled. "Just jam it on. The Styrofoam on the inside will deform if you force it. And it'll make it a little bit bigger for Sarah when she wears it again. She said it felt a little snug."

Dean looked crooked at Jim.

"Seriously," said Jim still smiling.

Dean forced the helmet onto his head. He had to remove it to adjust the strap so it would fasten under his chin. Hal took Dean's chin into his hand and moved his head from side to side inspecting the helmet. Then he grabbed both sides of the helmet and tried to wiggle it.

"It'll do." Hal picked up Dean's rope. "I'll take this. You get the rest of your gear on and meet us outside."

Dean came out of the barn wearing Sarah's helmet, his chaps, a glove on his left hand and his vest. Hal and Jim were by the steer penned off alone. Nell and Sarah stood watching. Charlie from Gus' ranch were there also. Hal stood on the lower rail of the fence and had Dean's rope wrapped around the steer's chest. He held onto the rope so it wouldn't fall off. The steer also had a rope tied around its flank which lay up against its hind legs.

"You want me to ride the steer?"

"You ever ride a bull before?"

"No."

"I've never seen you ride anything, not even a horse. If we had a mechanical bull, I'd start you out on that and work up."

"I've ridden a mechanical bull."

"Good. Today you'll ride a steer."

Dean looked over at Nell and the others. "It's embarrassing."

"Like throwing up before every ride?"

"Well..."

"Did you throw up before riding the mechanical bull?"

"No."

"Does the thought of riding the steer make you feel like you're going to throw up?"

"No."

"Ride the steer. If you do okay, you can ride the bull next time."

Dean climbed up on the fence next to Hal who still held the rope snug around the steer's chest.

"Ease onto him and I'll give you the rope. Jim, will you be latch man?"

"Wire man?" said Jim.

"Yeah, that."

Dean hesitated.

"He's not a bull. But he is a good step above a mechanical ride. He'll turn faster and sharper than the machine. And he's alive. So this is a natural progression for you. He won't buck as hard as a bull, but he will buck 'cause he's got that flank rope on and he hates it. So just ease onto him and we'll wait 'til you're ready."

Dean put his right leg over the steer's back and eased down until the animal held his full weight. Hal waited until Dean took hold of the rope before he let go.

"Make sure it's tight. Your wrangler will help you get the rope tight. If you don't like it that tight or want it tighter, say so."

Dean adjusted the rope and squeezed it back on itself with his left hand.

"Good. Now grip him with your knees and legs and I don't want to see daylight between your butt and the steer's back. Get your package right up against that rope. Once the bull's moving, all this goes right out the window."

Dean nodded.

"Okay," said Hal.

Dean shifted his weight forward and gripped the rope tighter.

"Go, Dean." Dean looked up and saw Sarah waving from the sidelines and Nell and Charlie were giving him thumbs up.

"Looks good." Hal looked at Dean. Dean stared at the steer's back. "Keep your right hand up off the bull. Pretend you're waving to the crowd."

Jim looked at Dean. Dean stared at the steer's back.

Hal straightened up on the fence and fished a stopwatch out of his pocket. "Eight seconds."

Dean still stared at the steer's back.

"He won't go until you nod to your latch man."

"Wire man," said Dean.

"Yeah, him."

Dean took a deep breath, looked to Jim and nodded. Jim opened the gate. Hal pushed the button on the stopwatch.

The steer didn't move.

For a full second the steer just sat there. And then it lurched out of the pen. It took two steps and tried to kick off the flank rope and Dean along with it. Dean held on but his butt flew well above the steer's back and the impact, when his butt came back down, sent him flying. He landed in the dirt and rolled away.

The steer ran off and Dean picked himself up out of the dust and returned to Hal. Sarah, Nell and Charlie were cheering. "Yay, Dean," yelled Sarah.

Hal checked the stopwatch, "Three seconds."

"Three seconds? That's all?" said Dean

"I'd call that pretty good for a first ride."

"But only three seconds."

"For a first ride. You want to go again?"

Dean thought about it for only a moment, "Yep."

"Charlie, will you help us get the steer back into the pen?"

"Sure."

"You relax a bit," Hal said to Dean.

Hal, Jim and Charlie herded the steer back toward the pen. They worked to get him facing the right direction so he'd come out correctly when the gate opened. Dean went over to Nell and Sarah while he waited.

"That was awesome," said Sarah.

"Nice ride," said Nell.

"Three seconds."

"Three long seconds."

"And you looked great all the time you were on him," said Sarah.

"That you did," said Nell. "How you feeling?"

"Okay."

"Really?"

"Really."

"Good. 'Cause it looks like they're ready for

you."

Jim wired the gate shut and Charlie and Hal climbed over the fence. Dean went over to the pen.

"This time he'll be more tired," said Hal.

"Really?"

"At least three seconds worth," said Hal. "And he'll be a little bit used to your weight. But he's still going to hate that flank rope so don't expect an easy ride."

"I won't."

"Good. You know what to do."

Hal held the rope while Dean eased on to the steer's back. When seated, Hal passed the rope to him. Hal pulled out the stopwatch and straightened up. "All yours."

Dean didn't hesitate this time. He looked at Jim and nodded. Jim opened the gate and Hal pressed the stopwatch.

The steer didn't wait either. It came out of the gate and bucked right away to rid itself of the flank rope and the rider.

Dean held the rope as tight as he could and squeezed the steer with his knees. Wilder and more unpredictable than the mechanical bull, the steer bucked his knees loose for a moment. Dean came back down still on the steer's back and squeezed his knees tighter. His right hand jerked back and forth above his head. He managed a very brief wave to Sarah and Nell. He wasn't sure they could even tell.

"Time," shouted Hal.

On the next landing, Dean threw one leg over the steer's back and dropped to the ground. The momentum carried him off his feet but he tucked his head and rolled back up. He watched the steer run off and headed over to Hal.

"Yay, Dean," Sarah yelled. Charlie whistled and Nell clapped.

In the adjacent pen, the bull snorted.

TWELVE

"Sarah, go tell Hal it's time for lunch."

Sarah went out the door. She didn't see Hal and tried the barn. "Hal." No one answered so she climbed up the stairs to his room. The door was ajar so she pushed it open. "Hal, you home?"

She spotted Hal's rucksack poking out from under the bed. The top lay open and something metal glinted. She pulled it out. It was a spur. Tarnished and dull, it looked like it might have been very pretty once. She pulled the rucksack further open and found the spur's partner in the same condition.

Hal's boots sounded on the steps. Sarah put the spurs back in the rucksack and pushed it under the bed.

"Your mom said you'd be out here."

"I was just looking."

"It's okay."

"You have spurs."

"Spurs?"

"I saw them."

"Ah, my spurs. Yeah, they're the only part of my kit I still have."

"They're rusty."

"That's 'cause they're old."

"Why don't you wear them?"

"I don't need 'em no more. Let's go get lunch."

"Why don't you need them anymore?" said Sarah at the lunch table.

"Need what?" said Jim

"The spurs."

"What spurs?"

"Hal's spurs."

"Hal, you holding out on us?" said Nell.

"They're just an old set of irons. Don't mean nothing."

"I saw them in Hal's room."

Jim looked at Sarah and then at Hal. "Can I see them?"

"They're not much to look at."

"Still. I'd like to see them."

Jim turned the spur over in his hand. He rubbed the yoke and spun the rowel with his thumb and then did the same for the other spur. Sarah watched her father as he rubbed the spur before he looked up at Hal.

"They're a bit rusted," said Hal.

"This isn't rust." Jim looked again at Hal who didn't answer.

Hal shrugged.

"And these aren't iron spurs or even steel. These are award spurs. Silver. The kind they give you when you win the All-Around."

Hal looked at Jim then at Sarah.

"You're name was familiar to me when we met on the road last summer. I thought it was just the name of the old mine. I remembered when I saw you on the horse at Gus'. Now, I'm sure. I know who you are. You're Gene Henry Comstock."

Hal looked down.

"I watched you ride. I was there. I saw you fall."

"Long time ago."

"Why did you stop competing?"

"Too old. Too out of practice. Took too long to heal."

Jim rubs at the spurs. "You were what, twenty-seven, twenty-eight when that bull threw you? That makes you forty-one now? Forty-two tops?"

"Forty-two is old for a bull rider. Forty-two is old for any kind of rough stock rider, let alone bulls."

Jim still rubs at the spurs. "These aren't rusted. Silver doesn't rust. These are tarnished. You should clean 'em up and wear 'em."

"They'll just rust -- tarnish -- again."

"Not if you use 'em. You gotta use 'em to keep 'em shiny."

THIRTEEN

Hal watched as Sarah rode Blackie around the corral, now with a saddle. He had set up three plastic barrels in a triangle pattern. She trotted the horse in a looping figure eight pattern around all three. Jim came up and stood beside Hal and watched Sarah ride.

"Awful small pattern."

"It fits our little arena. Later, we'll move the barrels out of the corral and get them regulation distance apart. For now she's still practicing control and turns. And for that, smaller is better."

"You got her roping from horseback yet?"

"Just started throwing for the post."

"Can she practice without you?"

"Sure. She knows how. Now it's just putting in the time to get it right. After that we'll start on calves."

"Good. You remember me telling you about my neighbor?"

"Yes, but I don't remember her name."

"Jenet."

"That's right."

"I've talked to her and she could use some

help around her place. Wages are the same so you'll be earning some extra money for the extra time. If you're agreeable, you'll work Monday, Wednesday and Friday for Jenet and the rest of the week here. You'll still get Sundays off."

"What does she need done?"

"Pretty much what you do here. Except there's no one you'll have to teach."

Hal borrowed one of Jim's horses for the ride to the Martin ranch. It had the same rolling terrain as Jim's ranch but twice the acreage. Hal tied the horse to one of the porch posts. Jenet Martin opened the door before he could knock.

"You must be Hal." She stepped forward and held out her hand.

"Yes, ma'am."

"Come on in." She held the door for him. He wiped his boots on the mat before entering.

"Would you like a drink?" she said as Hal followed her to the kitchen. "All I have is ice tea or lemonade at the moment."

"Lemonade would be fine."

"I understand you like beer, but I'm all out. My son visited this weekend and he finished off what I had."

"Lemonade is great."

Jenet poured two glasses of lemonade from an iced pitcher and brought the glasses to the table. Hal took a long sip.

"Careful, you'll get brain freeze."

Hal laughed. "I don't really get that."

"Brain freeze?"

"No."

"I wonder why that is? You'd better be careful. Some doctor will want to experiment on you to see what makes you different."

"I think alcohol acts like anti-freeze."

Jenet looked at Hal and laughed. "Alcohol as anti-freeze. Well said."

"Ma'am?"

"Tell me, Hal, do I shock you?"

"No, ma'am."

"Yes I do. I saw the way you looked when I mentioned the beer. I heard all about your wild ride at Gus' Fourth of July picnic. I didn't see it. You were on the ground before I got to the corral."

"I missed it, too."

"So I heard." Jenet laughed again. "I think we'll get along fine."

Hal took another drink from his glass.

FOURTEEN

Sarah came home from a shopping trip to town with her mom to find the blacksmith's truck parked by the corral. She looked at Nell who nodded. Sarah handed her the bag she carried and ran to the barn.

Inside, she found the blacksmith, Hector, working on her horse. Hal held Blackie's foreleg up while Hector checked to see that the shoe fit. Hal looked up as Sarah came in but didn't release the horse's leg.

"Thought it was time to dress him proper."

"He's never had shoes before."

"He was wild," said Hector. "Now, he's not."

Sarah picked up one of the horseshoes stacked on top of the railing. "If wild horses don't need shoes, why do tame ones?"

Hector crouched down and took Blackie's foreleg onto his knee. Hal stood and stroked the horse's forehead.

"Come and talk to him," said Hal.

Sarah hung the horseshoe over a nail on the post.

Hal went to the horseshoe Sarah had just

hung up and took it off the nail. "You shouldn't hang 'em like that."

"Sorry."

"No need. Just and old cowboy superstition."

Sarah looked at Hal.

"You can stack horseshoes or lay them flat," said Hector. "But, if you hang them, never hang them open-side down. All your luck will run out. You want to hang them like this." He showed her the horseshoe he was working with the open side up.

"How do you do that with only one nail?"

Hal laughed.

"That's the trick of it," said Hector.

Sarah went to stand by Blackie's head and kissed him on the forehead. "Sorry, Blackie. I don't want to bring you any bad luck."

Hector took a nail and tapped it into the shoe he was working until it set and then hammered it all the way in. He did this with several more nails until the shoe held tight on Blackie's hoof.

"You asked why tame horses need shoes when wild ones don't," said Hector. "Wild horses run on harder ground. With all that running, they don't really need shoes."

"Wouldn't the harder ground make shoes more necessary?"

"You'd think so. But it's the other way around. The hard ground makes the nail wear down naturally and makes it stronger."

"And they don't stand around in all this muck," said Hal motioning toward the stables. "It's bad for the hooves."

"So the ground is softer here than if he was free?"

"Yes, much more so."

"The more a horse runs and the harder the ground, the less he needs a shoe for protection," said Hector. "It's a harder way, but healthier. Makes him *macho*."

Hector finished up the last of the shoes for Blackie and Hal untied the horse and held out the lead for Sarah.

"Will you walk him? He needs to try out his new shoes."

Sarah laughed and led Blackie out of the barn and into the sunlight.

FIFTEEN

"Show me a hondo," said Hal a few days later as he handed Sarah a coil of rope. He held Blackie's reins in his other hand. Blackie stood, saddled and ready to go. Sarah tied the knot quickly.

"Now the bowline."

She tied that one as well. Hal walked toward the post she used for target practice when throwing the rope.

"Show me you can rope the post."

She hit it.

"Again."

She coiled the rope and hit it again.

"Again."

She hit it a third time. Hal took the rope from her and looked at it carefully all along its length. Then took her hands and turned them over to look at her palms.

"Good. Which knot do you like better?"

"I like 'em both."

"Which one do you use most?"

"Probably the bowline."

"Stick with that one then until someone

says otherwise."

"Okay."

"Okay, then. Up."

Sarah put her foot into the stirrup and hoisted herself onto the horse's back. Hal handed her the reins and then the rope. He adjusted her foot in the stirrup.

"Now, hit it again."

Sarah roped the post.

"Good. Once more."

She coiled the rope, took aim and made it again.

"Now, do it while walking the horse."

Sarah clicked her tongue and nudged Blackie with her heels and he walked forward. She swung the rope over her head and let fly. The noose dropped over the post and she pulled it tight.

"Good. Come with me."

He led her to the corral which today held only a calf. Hal opened the gate and Sarah walked Blackie in.

"Just walk him. The calf will be shy enough without Blackie chasing him. He's going to keep moving away from you although much slower than in a competition. Just see if you can get the rope over his head."

Sarah and Blackie walked toward the calf who moved away, just as Hal had said. She resisted the urge to chase him and kept Blackie to a gentle walk. When she swung the rope over her head, the calf sped up. She threw anyway and the rope fell short.

"Good. Try again."

Sarah coiled the rope as Blackie kept walking behind the calf who had slowed down again.

"One of the hard things about roping a moving target is judging the distance. Both you and your target are moving so the distance between you two can keep changing. That's what just happened. You want your horse moving at the same speed as the calf so the distance between the two remains constant when you throw. You can also compensate by throwing farther. Aim ahead of the calf. Try it again."

She waited until the calf looked away before swinging the rope but she missed again.

"This is hard to do."

"And it'll get even harder as your speed increases. In a competition, that calf will bolt out of the chute at full run and it'll change direction and speed to keep away from you. That's where a good roping horse will save you. It'll learn to change speed and direction to keep you within striking distance of that calf no matter how it turns."

Sarah patted Blackie's neck and then leaned forward to whisper in his hear, "Don't worry, you'll be great."

"Try again," said Hal.

SIXTEEN

Hal forked the last of the straw into the stable for the horses and hung up the pitchfork. He came out of the stable leading the loaner horse from Jim that he rode when working for Jenet Martin. Jenet came out onto the porch carrying two bottles. She handed one to Hal.

"Figured it was hot enough for a beer, today."

"I won't say no."

He tipped the bottle up and drank. Jenet sipped at hers.

"I keep two bottles of beer in the fridge. You're welcome to help yourself."

Hal sipped his beer.

"We're not all Jim Rhodes."

"No ma'am. You sure aren't."

SEVENTEEN

"Let's have a look," called Hal from outside the barn. Nell and Sarah stood beside him and Charlie behind them. He would act as safety in the corral for Dean's ride. Jim came over from the corral where the bull, Snodgrass stayed penned in the makeshift chute. Dean came out of the barn wearing his bull-riding gear including the recently purchased helmet.

"It looks almost as good as mine," said Sarah.

"If feels a whole lot better than yours," said Dean.

Hal stepped forward and did a circuit around Dean. "Well, you certainly look like a bull rider."

He stopped in front of Dean and took hold of the helmet and tested the fit and then leaned in close, "How do you feel?"

Dean raised one eyebrow and shrugged and put one hand on his stomach. "I didn't know I had anything inside my stomach, but I guess I did."

"Okay, then," said Hal. "You ready?"

"Never more."

"Ride 'em, cowboy," said Nell as Dean and Hal walked past.

"Go, Dean. You can do it," said Sarah.

Dean handed the rope to Hal who climbed on the fence outside of the bull pen. He dropped on end onto the ground. Dean tossed the ground end under the bull to Charlie on the gate side. He lifted the rope to Jim who tossed the end back to Hal. Now, once around the bull, Hal looped the rope back on itself and held it for Dean.

Dean climbed the fence and eased down on the bull's back. The bull shivered.

Charlie walked out to the middle of the corral. He carried a small white dish towel in one hand.

"Cinch up tight," said Hal.

The bull settled down. Jim undid the wire but held the gate shut.

Nell and Sarah waited at the fence.

"Eight seconds," said Hal.

Dean nodded to him.

"Ride 'em, cowboy."

Dean looked directly at Jim and nodded. Jim pulled the gate and stepped aside as the bull jerked sideways out of the pen with Dean hanging on.

The bull made the steer seem tame. Where the steer had been big, the bull seemed like a mountain. The bull bucked high and changed direction every time he hit the ground. Every move was like a whiplash.

Dean didn't know how long the ride lasted, but he lay on the ground and dust particles floated around his head. The bull trotted away from him toward Charlie who waved the dish towel. Charlie scrambled for the fence as the bull approached.

Dean picked himself up. Nell and Sarah were cheering. He headed over to the pen where Hal and Jim waited on the outside of the fence.

"Always watch the bull," said Hal, pointing.

Dean looked back and saw the bull looking at him. On the other side, Charlie scrambled over the fence. The bull didn't move but watched Dean. Dean backed up to the fence and then turned and climbed over.

"Good ride," said Jim shaking Dean's hand. "Good first ride."

"How long?"

Sarah and Nell were there. Charlie came around the corral.

"Doesn't matter," said Hal. "You got on and you rode a bull. There's not everyone can say that."

Sarah and Nell took turns hugging him. Charlie pumped his hand and said, "What a ride."

"Let's celebrate," said Nell. "Lemonade for everyone in the kitchen."

Dean unfastened his helmet as he and Sarah, Nell, and Charlie headed for the kitchen. Hal hung back and Jim stopped next to him. "You heading in?" Jim motioned after the others.

"In a second," said Hal. "I'm going to pick

up first."

He turned back to the corral and climbed the fence. Dean's rope lay inside a few feet from the pen. The bull stood at the far end watching him. Hal picked up the rope and tossed it to Jim.

"Want to help me get him back to the pen?" said Hal.

"Dean going to ride again?"

"No, I think one time is enough for today. I just want to get the flank rope off the bull. No need to keep him irritated."

The two herded the bull back to the pen and closed the gate. Once there, Hal loosened the flank rope and let it drop. Jim opened the gate again and the bull trotted out to the more open corral. Hal retrieved the rope and the two men climbed over the fence.

Hal left the flank rope in the barn but took Dean's rope with him as the two men walked to the kitchen where they could hear the others laughing.

"You going to tell me how long?"

Hal pulled the stopwatch out of his pocket and handed it to Jim who looked at it. "Two point two seconds."

"Good first ride."

"Yeah."

EIGHTEEN

Hal wiped the sweat from the back of his neck with his bandana. He had driven Jenet's battered pickup truck into town to pick up some bales of straw for her horses. He stacked six bales in the bed and drove down the main street on the way back watching as individual stalks flew off the back. Driving down the quiet business district, he passed a bar by the name of "Rusty's" with a lit neon open sign. He found a parking spot two doors down.

"What can I get you?" said the bartender as Hal sat down at the bar.

"You have Modelo?"

"Not draft."

"Bottle's fine."

"Negra?"

Hal nodded.

The bartender placed a dark bottle in front on the wood in front of Hal. Drops condensed and ran down the side of the wet bottle and pooled at the base. Hal picked it up and wiped the water on the bar with his free hand. He sipped the beer at first and then took a long drink.

"You that cowboy working for Jim Rhodes?"

"Yeah."

"But you're driving Jenet Martin's truck?"

"I do some work for her, too. The bales are for her."

"No big deal. You ride?"

"Horses?"

"Horses, bulls, whatever?"

"Not so much."

"Me, neither. I sort of limit myself to pickup trucks, now."

Hal tipped the bottle to him and drank again.

"You coming to the rodeo?"

"Don't know anything about it."

"Just put the sign up." He pointed to the poster at the far end of the bar. "Still a month out. Local only but we like to get a good turnout."

"I'll be there," said Hal. He finished the beer and put five dollars on the bar and set the bottle on top.

"See you."

"It's an annual thing," said Jenet. "The Bowman Roundup. We're pretty small. Sort of a sideshow on the circuit. But all the locals get to show off a little bit."

"I'm thinking for Sarah."

"Is she ready to compete?"

"She's close. She's good at the barrel racing.

She's tight on those corners. She's fair with roping. She hasn't got the size for a tie-down, yet. But she could do fair in a breakaway. Maybe in another month, she'll be ready."

"It sounds like she learns pretty quick."

"She has the want."

"Good. Well, you can buy me a beer at the roundup."

"I'll do that. Mrs. Martin?"

"Call me Jenet."

"Yes, ma'am – Jenet. Would it be okay if I made a phone call?"

"Why, sure."

"It's to Stephenville."

"Is that where you're from, Hal?"

"One of many."

"You can use the phone in the bedroom. It'll give you a bit of privacy."

Hal went into the bedroom and sat on the bed but didn't close the door. He pushed the numbers on the phone and waited.

"Hello?"

"Hello?" said the voice in his ear.

"Hey, it's me." Through the open door, Jenet could hear his voice soften.

He listened for a moment and then said, "I'm okay. I'm doing okay."

Jenet went to the bedroom and pulled the door closed. Hal looked up at her and mouthed the word, "Thanks."

"Exes never really do go away, do they?" said Jenet.

"Sorry 'bout that."

"No, no."

"Pretty obvious, huh?"

"Some of it. I didn't hear much. What's her name?"

"Lizbeth."

"How long since you seen her?"

"Been a while, now. A few years. I call her once in a while to check in and see how she's doing."

"Still miss her?"

"Sometimes, yeah." He motioned toward his ear. "It may get quieter now and then, but the ringing never really goes away."

NINETEEN

Sarah and Blackie trotted around the corral. Jim held the calf in the pen and Hal waited by the gate. Sarah stopped Blackie next to Hal. He held the dish towel that Charlie had waved when Dean rode the bull. A heavy string tied around the middle of the towel extended out about eighteen inches. A lighter string, tied to the first string, led out about eighteen inches in the opposite direction.

"Here's the thing about the breakaway." He tied one end of the heavier string tightly around the rope. "You don't want to tie the string too close to the noose 'cause you might throw too short and miss the calf entirely." He tied the lighter string around the saddle horn. "But if you tie it too far down the rope, the calf gets to run farther before it breaks this string and your time goes up. And in this event, everything's about the time. Understand?"

"Yes."

"The judges won't look at how pretty you ride or how well you handle your rope. It's the clock you're trying to impress. Lowest number on the clock, wins."

"Then what are the judges there for?"

"They'll tell us whether we can count your time – whether you committed a foul or something." Hal watched her. "The clock, yes?"

"Yes."

"Good." Hal motioned toward the rope still in his hands. "This is about the middle and about where you've been practicing. Later you can adjust where on the rope you tie the string."

"In a competition, there's a chute which the calf comes out of. We don't have one, so we improvise." He paced out eight steps and used the heel of his boot to carve a line in the dirt. "The calf also gets a head start, usually about twenty-eight feet." He indicated the line. "You don't get to start until the calf reaches this line. In the rodeo, it'll be mechanical. There'll be a breakaway collar on the calf attached to a rope. When the calf gets to the end of the rope it will trigger the barrier to drop and the collar will fall off the calf along with the rope. So far so good?"

"Yes."

"You and Blackie will be in a box next to the chute with the calf. The end facing the arena is open but there will be a rope across the opening with a flag in the middle. You can't hit that rope before it drops otherwise there's a ten second penalty and that penalty will knock you out of the competition."

"Okay."

"Since we don't have the box or rope, I'm just going to hold the bridle. Later on we'll practice timing your run up to the rope."

"Got it."

"Okay. Jim you ready?" he said as he took hold of Blackie's bridle.

"Yep."

"All right. Let him go."

Jim opened the gate. The calf trotted out. When it passed him, Jim slapped it on the rump. The calf bolted forward and reached the line a second later.

Hal released the bridle and pressed the stopwatch. Sarah yelled and Blackie surged forward after the calf.

The calf reached the fence on the other side and then veered left to circle the corral. He made it almost a full circuit when Sarah launched the rope and pulled back on the reins. Blackie stopped but the calf kept running, pulling the rope taut. The string tied to the saddle horn broke and the dish towel flapped behind the calf as it kept running. Sarah and Blackie trotted back to the pen.

"Well done," said Jim.

"Fourteen seconds," said Hal.

"Is that good?"

"You'll get faster."

"How fast should she be?" said Jim.

Hal shrugged. "A professional calf roper can rope and tie the calf in seven or eight seconds. This is the breakaway. Last I heard the world record was under two seconds."

"Two seconds?"

"For a world record."

"How fast should she be?"

"As fast as she can."

"Can I go again?" said Sarah still on her horse.

"Sure. Let's get your rope back from the calf."

With the calf back in the pen, Sarah coiled the rope tied the string to the saddle horn. Jim opened the gate again. This time the calf didn't wait but ran as soon as it could clear the gate. Hal released the bridle at the line and Sarah and Blackie charged after the calf with Sarah swinging the rope over her head. The calf made it about three quarters of the circle when Sarah threw.

The rope bounced off the calf and fell to the ground.

Blackie came to a stop and the calf, no longer pursued, slowed down and found a spot on the other side of the corral.

"Everybody misses," said Hal. "Go again."

Sarah roped the calf twice more, once in fourteen seconds and once in twelve.

TWENTY

Dean waited by the fire with the iron while Charlie and Adam brought a calf over and laid it down. Charlie held it while Adam circled the rope around its legs. The Gustafson mark consisted of two "G's" that faced each other. Dean used the hot iron to put the brand on the animal's rump. Then Adam untied the legs and the calf sprinted off. Charlie led the next one to the fire.

Gus pulled up in his truck and watched them as they branded the last calf. "How many is that?" he said from the driver's seat.

"Seventeen," said Adam. "I think we got all of them on this side."

"We'll work the other end, tomorrow," said Charlie.

"Good. Ride back in with me, Dean."

Dean handed Charlie the keys to the truck they'd come out in and headed over to his father's truck. He opened the door and climbed into the passenger seat and Gus drove off down the dirt trail.

"I heard you rode a bull."

"Yeah, but not long."

"Well, time's relative according to Einstein."

Dean laughed. "But not according to the PBR."

Gus laughed in his turn. "I guess they never heard of Einstein. But you did ride."

"Yeah."

Gus reached over and grabbed Dean's forearm. "Good job."

"Thanks, Dad."

"You going to ride in the rodeo?"

"I'm not sure."

"What's the hold up?"

"I've been on exactly one bull for a total of two seconds. I don't think I'm ready for the circuit."

"Oh, I'm not talking about the circuit or even a regional. I do think you should ride in the Roundup, though."

"It's only a couple of weeks away."

"So ride the bull again for practice and sign up."

"Maybe."

"Maybe. It really only counts in a competition if you make it eight full seconds on the bull."

"That's a long way off from where I sit and I may never get there."

"Yeah, your mom told me."

"That I want to be a bullfighter?"

"Yeah."

"You are."

"Yeah. But I was a bull rider first."

They sat for a few moments as Gus left a cloud of dust on the road behind them.

"How are things with that Hal?"

"Hal? He sure knows his stuff about rodeo."

"For instance?"

"He's taught Sarah a lot about roping and riding. He seems to know a lot about both rough stock and time trials."

"Did he ride Snodgrass?"

"No. At least not that I saw. Why?"

"Just wondering is all."

TWENTY-ONE

At two in the morning, Hal came down the stairs from his room above the barn fully dressed except for his feet. On those, he wore only his socks. He stopped at the bottom of the stairs to pull on his boots. He came out the door and pulled open one of adjacent barn doors. The hinge on the door squeaked. The same hinge that squeaked the first morning he worked for Jim Rhodes. He stared for a moment at the hinge and then looked back toward the main house. Nothing stirred. He went into the barn but left the door open. He returned a moment later with the oil can and oiled the hinge. He pulled the door closed behind him and latched it.

At the end of the barn, past Blackie's stall, Snodgrass waited. He snorted at Hal when he saw him.

"Did you see me first or smell me?"

Snodgrass breathed heavy and eyed Hal. Hal ran a hand down the bull's back from behind the head all the way to the base of his tail. The bull shuddered slightly. Hal reached under the bull's chin and scratched. The bull huffed and turned his head toward Hal and then dropped his head and butted the rail. Hal scratched the bull's forehead.

"Easy, now."

Hal dropped a heavy leather halter over the bull's head and fastened it with the lead to the left of the bull's head. He attached a second rope using a snap swivel to the right side of the halter. Hal opened the latch to the stall and led the animal out of the barn and into the corral.

Hal stopped the bull next to the fence and used it to climb up. He had both leads in his left hand and lifted his left leg over the bull's back. When the bull moved forward, Hal pulled on the leads a bit and the bull stopped. Hal settled down on the bull's back. The bull shuddered again.

"Easy, now. Easy, big fella." Hal patted the bull on the back with his free hand and scratched him on his neck.

When the bull settled, Hal clicked his tongue and shook the ropes. He kept his heels away from the bull and gripped the bull's sides only with his knees.

The bull walked forward. Hal used the ropes as reins and kept the bull near the fence. In this way, at a walking pace, they made a complete circuit of the corral. Hal made another circle with the bull and then slipped his leg across the bull's back and dropped to the ground. He led the bull back into the barn and to his stable where he removed the halter and scratched the bull one more time under the chin.

"Yeah, you're nothing but a two-thousand pound lamb."

The bull snorted.

"Okay, maybe not a lamb."

Hal undid the swivel snap and separated the extra line from the halter. He removed the halter and hung both on hooks near the bull's stall and turned back to the bull.

"I do think we are going to have to figure out new name for you, Lamb Chop."

The bull huffed.

Hal closed the barn door which did not squeak this time. He turned to go upstairs to his room and glanced back at the main house. There, in an upstairs window, he saw Sarah watching him.

The barrels were outside the corral and set up at regulation distance from each other. Sarah rode hard at the first barrel and Blackie made the first turn just brushing the barrel. It wobbled but didn't fall. Hal nodded as he watched her ride.

Sarah kept Blackie tight on the second barrel as well. He made the turn and charged for the third barrel at the top of the pattern. He looped too wide around it and lost some time. Sarah and Blackie now charged for the finish line where Hal waited.

"Eighteen seconds," said Hal, looking at his stopwatch.

"Eighteen," said Sarah patting Blackie.

Hal handed her the stopwatch. "Keep going and come get me when you get to fifteen."

"Hal?"

Hal waited.

"Will you teach me how to ride a bull?"

Hal looked at her for a moment while taking Blackie's bridle. "You mean like I rode the bull or like dean rode the bull?"

She waited a moment before she answered, "Both."

"There are some ladies who ride bulls, but not many. It's a rough sport. People get hurt."

"It didn't look dangerous when you rode."

"He didn't have a flank rope."

"Is that the difference?"

"It's one of the things that makes a difference." Hal reached up and stroked the black horse's forehead. "Everyone thinks bulls are just mean by nature. But that's not right. They're herd animals just like horses."

"They want to be part of a herd?"

"Horses want to make friends with everyone. Just like this guy. Bulls not so much. Bulls want to make friends with their own kind and not really anybody else. Everyone else is an enemy."

"Really."

"It's more than that. It's about defense. Horses and bulls will both choose to run away from any threat in the wild. But horses run faster. They can kick and bite and trample, but by and large, the better horses just run faster. And horses will always run first. Bulls will run, too. But bulls aren't as fast and can't sustain the run for as long. So when they can't run any more, or they're cornered, or they're protecting a calf, well then they have their horns."

"It makes me feel sorry for the bulls."

"Me, too."

"What you did last night, will it make Snodgrass too tame to ride?"

"You mean for Dean?"

"Or anyone else."

"No. As soon as you put a flank rope on him and a rider on his back, he'll see the rider as his enemy. They have other tricks, too, for amping up a bull in a competition. Put the bull alone in a pen. Take away his friends."

"Don't the bull riders hate that?"

"No. You get a bigger score for riding a tougher bull. Judges and riders like that. Point is, if you want to make the bull crazy, and go for the big points in a rodeo, put him in a pen by himself and then put the flank rope on him."

"But you're not trying to make him crazy. Are you?"

"No."

"Are you practicing to ride again?"

"No."

"Then why did you ride him?"

Hal looked at the ground and shrugged. "Come and get me when you hit fifteen."

TWENTY-TWO

The Bowman Roundup took place the last Saturday in October every year. With the weather not yet cold, and the heat of the summer gone, it seemed the perfect time for relaxing and riding rodeo. It also gave the members of the community time to get together and have coffee and talk. Sort of like after church on Sunday mornings.

Jim and Nell walked through the small midway heading toward the arena. The midway held stalls selling food and craft goods and souvenirs. But the main attraction was the rodeo where local cowboys and cowgirls got to compete and display their skills.

"I hear we're going to see Sarah throwing her rope," said Gus as he and Abby came up.

"Yes," said Nell. "And I saw Dean on the list to ride."

"Fingers crossed," said Abby.

"Bull riding is the last event," said Gus. "So he's going to have to wait through it all. Where's Hal?"

"He's with Sarah," said Jim.

"Will we see Dean before he rides?" said Nell.

"Maybe," said Abby.

"I doubt it," said Gus. "He's probably tucked up somewhere, sweating."

"I remember when you used to ride," said Abby. "You were the same as Dean."

"Yeah, I know. I don't blame him for it. I'm sure he gets it from me."

"You should let him know that."

"You don't think he does?"

"It would be nice for him to hear from his father."

"You want to sit with us?" said Jim as they reached the entrance to the arena.

The bleachers were only about half full. People trickled in. The bleachers would be full by the time the rough stock events came up. On the arena floor, some clowns in bright face paint scrambled around and performed gags for the audience. Abby gave Gus a look.

"Stop it," said Gus.

"What?"

"You know what."

"What are you two discussing?" said Nell.

"Gus and I are having a longstanding discussion about what makes a rodeo clown a rodeo clown and what makes a bullfighter a bullfighter?"

One of the clowns brought a boy who looked to be about five years old into the arena. The boy wore a vest, chaps and a helmet. He lifted the boy over the fence into the chute where a sheep waited. Another clown in the chute helped the boy settle himself on the sheep.

"Ladies and gentlemen," said the announcer. Directing your attention to the ring where Chris Williams is making his first ever rodeo ride."

The audience applauded. The latch man opened the gate and the sheep, with Chris clinging to its back, raced out. The boy buried his face in the wool as well as both hands. The sheep ran across the arena. It reached the other side and hesitated for a blink while trying to decide which direction to go for safety. One of the clowns in the arena shooed it and it ran the other way where another clown plucked Chris from its back and stood him up on the floor. The audience cheered and clapped.

"Let's hear it for Chris Williams," said the announcer. The audience cheered and clapped again and Chris threw his hands up in the air.

"I love these," said Abby. "These rides are so much fun."

"So what's the difference?" said Nell. "Clowns and bullfighters?"

Gus sighed.

"Apparently," said Abby, "rodeo clowns are just clowns that entertain the crowd while bullfighters are clowns that protect the riders."

"Exactly," said Gus. "And the clowns pay more attention to their makeup. You can tell which ones worked at it and which ones didn't care so much how they look."

"So the bullfighters are sloppier with their makeup?"

"Like some women I know."

"Ow," said Abby.

"Not you, dear."

"So were the clowns in the ring with the sheep really just clowns or were they bullfighters?" said Nell.

"Most likely bullfighters," said Jim.

"How can you tell the difference?"

"Besides the makeup? Clowns come out between rides," said Gus. "Bullfighters are in the arena during the ride and not just sitting on the fence."

"Even for a sheep?"

"Yes."

"Then why do bullfighters dress like clowns?"

"Tradition," said Jim. "Used to be all rodeo clowns were bullfighters and all bullfighters were rodeo clowns."

"Tradition is a big thing for cowboys, isn't it?" said Nell.

Gus nodded.

The first of the calf roping events were the breakaways. Sarah's event. The list showed her as the third rider. The first calf came out trailing a rope that released a barrier when the calf reached its head start distance. The first rider's horse balked in the box and came out late. Still, the rider roped the calf and the clock showed fifteen seconds flat. The second rider did better. She timed the barrier to the precise instant and her flag came off the saddle horn at just over eleven seconds.

"Eleven seconds is a good time," said Gus. "Has Sarah done that well in practice?"

"Close to it," said Jim. "But things are always different in a competition."

"Hush, you two," said Abby. "Here she comes."

Sarah rode Blackie into the ring and over to the box next to the chute. Hal got up on the fence next to her. The latch man fastened the rope barrier across the opening with the flag hanging down.

As the handlers loaded Sarah's calf into the chute, one of the bullfighters walked over to Hal and spoke to him. Hal nodded. The bullfighter stepped moved closer to Hal and held out his hand. Hal took it and the two shook hands.

"I think that guy knows Hal," said Gus.

"Maybe so," said Jim. "Do you know him?"

"That's Abraham Poole. He's been around for a long time. Follows the circuit."

"Hey," said Nell. "How come you're not out there in your makeup?"

"Me?" said Gus. "I'm a spectator today. Besides, I think it would make Dean even more nervous having me in the ring with him."

"Up next, Sarah Rhodes riding Black Works," said the announcer. "This is Sarah's first rodeo so let's wish her luck." The crowd applauded and then quieted. The bullfighter talking to Hal returned to his post in the arena.

The calf nosed the gate keeping it in the chute. It already looked nervous and would bolt the moment the gate swung open. Blackie stomped and then pawed at the ground. Sarah had Blackie as far back from the gate as the box allowed. She wanted as much a head start run as possible before hitting the rope. Sarah looked at Hal and he nodded.

Sarah nodded to the latch man. He swung the gate open and the calf bolted out stretching out the release rope. At two-thirds the distance to the release, Sarah clicked her tongue for Blackie. If she started too soon, they would hit the barrier before the calf had its full head start and take a penalty. If she waited too long, they would be too far behind the barrier and would lose time that way.

Blackie reached the barrier at a gallop and Sarah swung the rope over her head just as the calf reached the end of its release rope and the barrier flag dropped. She timed it perfect and Blackie charged out of the box at a full gallop. Sarah and Blackie closed the distance fast and Sarah threw the rope. The noose made it halfway around the calf's head. The calf jerked its head to the right and the rope dropped off the calf's shoulder and fell to the ground.

TWENTY-THREE

Sarah sat in the stands between her mother and father. Nell had her arm around Sarah's shoulders. The fastest time in the Breakaway competition so far had been a hair over ten seconds.

"Ten seconds. You would've beat that, I think," said Jim. "You came out of the box right on time and at speed. You would have beat that sure."

"Maybe," said Sarah. "But I missed."

"Everyone misses," said Nell.

Sarah shook her head.

"How about an ice cream?" said Jim.

"You're not going to stay for the tie-downs?" said Gus.

"We'll be back. We got time for a quick ice cream."

Sarah nodded and she and Jim left the stands and headed for the midway.

"Dean tells me Sarah's pretty good with that rope," said Abby.

"Yeah. She doesn't miss that often," said Nell. "She's practiced so much."

"It's her first competition. She'll do better in the barrel racing."

"I hope so."

Jim and Sarah stood in line for ice cream. They were four back from the front of the line. Jenet Martin got in line behind them.

"Hello, neighbors," said Jenet Martin.

"Jenet," said Jim. "We were watching the roping."

"I saw Sarah ride. Sorry about the throw, honey."

"Thank you."

"You'll get him next time."

"Barrel racing is her next event."

"I was a barrel racer," said Jenet.

"Yeah?"

"When I was younger. I remember competing against your mom at some rodeos."

"Really?"

"Really."

They were at the front of the line and Jim ordered three ice cream cones. He handed one to Sarah and one to Jenet and kept the third.

"Hey, there's Hal," said Sarah as they stepped away from the ice cream stand. "Hal. Hey, Hal."

Hal stood at the beer concession. He had a bottle in his hand. A pretty woman wearing boots, blue jeans and a cowboy hat stepped up to him. Hal turned at the sound of his name. He dropped his bottle into the trash can and waved. He took the woman's elbow and motioned toward

Sarah. They came over.

"Hal," said Jim.

"Jim, this is Lizbeth. Lizbeth, Jim Rhodes and Sarah. And this is Jenet Martin. I work at her ranch when I'm not working at Jim's."

Lizbeth held out a hand. "Jenet. Hal says nice things about you."

"Lizbeth?" said Jenet as she took Lizbeth's hand. "You're Hal's ex-wife?"

"Yes," smiled Lizbeth.

"Anyone seen Dean?" Gus called as he walked up to the group.

"Is he riding already?"

"No but they're calling the bull riders for check in."

"I'll see if I can find him," said Hal. "Lizbeth, I'll catch up with you later."

Hal and Gus went separate directions. Lizbeth smiled at Sarah. "I hear you're spot on with your rope."

"I missed today."

"Oh."

"We're heading back to watch the rest of the tie-downs," said Jim. "Would you like to join us?"

"Sorry, I'm actually going to meet someone."

"Another time, then."

"Absolutely."

"Nice to meet you," Lizbeth said to Jenet.

"And you."

Lizbeth walked away.

"Hal's ex-wife?" said Sarah.

Jim shrugged.

Hal walked back to the men's ready room. A few riders sat around trying to calm nerves. An ice chest sat in the corner. One rider sat with his shirt off on an examination table. Two other men manipulated his arm in a slow circular motion.

"Is it dislocated?"

"Probably a bad sprain."

"I can ride again?"

"Not today. Today we get x-rays to make sure."

"Anyone see Dean Gustafson?" Hal asked into the room.

The two medics turned and shook their heads. One of the seated riders spoke up.

"He left when the call came in."

"You see where he went?"

"Just out the door."

Hal went to the ice chest and took out a bottle of water. "If you see him, tell him I'm looking for him."

Hal went to the riders' meeting room next. He opened the door and poked his head in. He didn't see Dean and shut the door. He walked to the edge of the arena and scanned the bleachers. Across the arena from him sat Sarah and her family. He saw Gus and Abby with them but no Dean. He turned and walked back toward the stalls and pens. A few hands managed the animals.

"Dean Gustafson?"

"Cowboy?" asked one of the men.

"Yes. You seen him?"

The first man motioned with his head toward a second man. The second man came over.

"You looking for the cowboy?"

"Yes."

The man motioned over his shoulder. "In the barn. In the back."

"Much obliged."

"Careful where you step."

The arena held a long barn divided into stalls the entire length. Most of the stalls held horses waiting for their turn in the ring. The horses neighed and tossed their heads as Hal entered. They knew it was rodeo time and they were excited, too.

A stall near the far end of the barn looked empty. At least it did not hold a horse that Hal could see. He headed for that one.

Hal heard the retching before he reached the gate. He looked over the stall. Dean was on his hands and knees with his face low over the straw. He retched again while Hal watched but nothing came out of his mouth. Hal went to him and held out the bottle of water. Dean looked up at him and held up his hand.

"Don't think I can hold it down."

"Then just rinse and spit."

Dean took the bottle and unscrewed the lid. He poured a bit into his mouth and was on his knees gagging a second later. Hal took the bottle from him and waited until the episode passed.

"Again," said Hal holding out the bottle.

Dean waved him away.

"Again," said Hal. "And again, and again, and again."

TWENTY-FOUR

In the arena, the men were finishing the tie-down roping events. These guys were fast with some of the times nearing seven seconds.

"Up next, from Stephenville, Texas, Roy Morris," said the announcer.

A big man, Morris looked to be at least six foot eight. He rode a big horse, too, but Morris made him look like a pony when he was in the saddle. Horse and rider went into the box and Morris turned him around to face the flag. He backed the horse up all the way to the fence and waited in the saddle. The crowd got quiet.

Gus took his seat. "This guy's real good."

"You find Dean?"

"No."

"I'm sure he's around."

"Yeah."

Abby took Gus' hand.

"You know this guy?" said Jim.

"Yeah, he won the all-around at Fort Worth a few years ago. Retired for a while to heal up and now is starting to ride again."

Jim turned to Sarah, "Watch this guy. This

could be good."

The horse and rider in the box stood still. The crowd quieted. The horse huffed once and the rider put the tie-down string between his teeth and bit down and then nodded to the latch man.

The chute opened and the calf ran forward trailing its release rope. The rider and the horse waited. The rider nodded his head once, twice and then spurred his horse and swung the rope hard and fast around his head. Horse and rider shot forward toward the flag so fast Sarah thought they would break through the barrier before the flag dropped.

The calf reached the end of the rope and the collar dropped off together with the release rope causing the flag to drop just as the horse reached it. The horse already moved at a full charge. Its hooves pounded the turf as rider and horse chased the frightened calf.

Morris still swung the rope over his head. He threw the rope and pulled hard as his horse skittered to a stop while the calf kept running forward. The rope stretched tight and jerked the calf's head backward. Morris jumped from his horse before it stopped moving. The calf yelped as momentum carried the body and legs forward and the calf flipped over onto its back. The audience gasped at the loud crack as the calf's back hit the ground.

Morris ran to the calf with the tie-down string in his hand and stopped at the calf's side.

The calf twitched and made a frantic sound. Morris dropped to his knees and touched the calf's head with one hand and its flank with the other. Then he stood and backed away and motioned for the handlers. The tie-down string remained on the ground next to the calf.

The clock kept running.

Sarah dropped her ice cream onto the floorboards.

TWENTY-FIVE

Adam and Charlie sat at a table inside Rusty's bar with two other hands from the ranch with a half-empty bottle of beer in front of each. Adam sat facing the door so he was the first to see Lizbeth step through the door. He looked to Charlie and then back to the door and raised one eyebrow. Charlie turned to look as did Paul and Hector, the other two ranch hands. They all turned back to the table.

"Why do I know her?" said Charlie.

Paul shrugged.

"She was at the rodeo," said Hector.

Charlie looked back as Lizbeth took a seat at the bar. From his seat, Adam didn't have to turn to watch.

"I think she was," said Adam. "I saw her talking to that fella Hal from Jim Rhodes's place."

"She was talking to Hal?" said Charlie.

"She was," said Adam as he got to his feet. "And I'm going to buy her first beer."

"She's already drinking a beer."

"Well, then," said Adam.

Adam took his beer with him and sat down

at the empty stool next to Lizbeth and motioned to the bartender. "Let me pay for the lady's beer."

Lizbeth looked at Adam. "Too late. It's already paid for."

"Well, the next one then."

"What's your name, cowboy?"

"Adam. Let me guess – you're Eve?"

Lizbeth smiled. "You must have wrung that one dry a long time ago."

"Yeah, but I couldn't resist. Are you telling me it didn't work?"

"Adam, I'm flattered – really – but I'm expecting someone."

"Maybe he won't show."

"Oh, I think he will." She held out her hand. Adam took it. "Thank you, Adam. You're very sweet. But I think your friends are waiting for you." She nodded in the direction of the table where Charlie, Paul and Hector watched them.

Adam stood. "I never did learn your name."

"Lizbeth."

"Short for Elizabeth?"

"No, just Lizbeth. Lizbeth Arneson."

The door to the street opened and Hal came in still wearing the black shirt he wore to the Roundup that day.

"Maybe next time," said Adam.

"Maybe next time," said Lizbeth.

Hal saw Lizbeth at the bar and moved toward her. He saw Charlie and the boys at the table and waved. Charlie waved back. Adam and

Hal passed each other and Hal took the seat next to Lizbeth where Adam sat moments before and gave her a quick hug. Adam resumed his seat at the table with the other hands.

"Oh, well," said Paul.

"Oh, well what?" said Adam.

Paul raised his hands, "Sorry. No harm meant."

Hector pushed back from the table and stood. "Next round is on me." He headed toward the bar.

Charlie looked at Adam and then at the bar where Hal and Lizbeth now sat. He looked back at Adam and shrugged.

"What's that supposed to mean?" said Adam.

"Nothing," Charlie raised his hands. "Nothing at all."

The door to the street opened again and Roy Morris ducked his head as he came in. He wore a clean pair of jeans and a white button-down shirt. His sleeves were rolled down and a bolo tie finished it off.

Roy scanned the room and saw Lizbeth at the bar. He headed over just as Hector returned from the bar carrying four bottles.

Lizbeth saw Roy coming toward her and stood up. Hal stood when Lizbeth did. Roy bent down and gave Lizbeth a quick kiss on the cheek. He held out his hand for Hal. Hal shook it. All three sat at the bar with Hal and Roy on either side of Lizbeth.

"Now ain't you glad you're not in the middle of that?" said Charlie.

"And how," said Paul.

Adam said nothing but nursed his beer.

"Isn't that Roy Morris?" said Hector.

"I think so," said Paul. "That was something today at the tie-downs."

"He was out of the gate so quick and strong."

"That was a hard thing."

At the bar, Roy said something which caused Lizbeth to laugh. She touched her bottle to his. Hal looked down at the top of the bar.

"He would have won the all-around but for that calf," said Paul.

"It wasn't the calf's fault."

"Poor little thing," said Hector.

"He's six nine," said Paul

"I meant the calf," said Hector.

Across the room, Roy and Lizbeth talked to each other. Hal stayed quiet. After a few minutes, Lizbeth turned more to face Roy. Hal glanced at her and then looked back to his own drink. Adam and Charlie noticed the move as well. Paul and Hector now turned around in their seats to see what the focus was.

The conversation at the bar was no more than a murmur to the hands sitting at the table. After a couple of moments, Lizbeth laughed and said, loud enough for Charlie and his table to hear, "Hal does like his fillies." Roy laughed hard at that. Hal pushed back from the bar and took his feet facing Roy. Roy slid off his bar stool and faced Hal. Roy stood at least six inches taller than Hal. Charlie guessed he outweighed Hal by at least fifty pounds on top of the height advantage.

"And what?" said Roy.

Hal said nothing but his hands were balled into fists and held down at his side.

Roy lifted his chin and looked down at Hal.

Lizbeth jumped from her seat and stood between the two men but faced Hal. Everyone else in the bar got real quiet.

"Enough," said Lizbeth. "Enough."

Neither man moved.

"Stand down," she said to Hal.

Hal opened his fists and shook his hands. He pulled out his wallet and laid a five-dollar bill on the counter, put his empty bottle on top of it and walked to the door. Lizbeth and Roy watched him go.

Charlie got up from his table to follow Hal. As he walked by the bar, Lizbeth turned to Roy.

"I could have taken him," said Roy.

"The hell you could," said Lizbeth.

Charlie reached the sidewalk outside and looked around for Hal. A minute later, he heard an engine start and saw Jenet Martin's truck pull out into the street and drive off.

TWENTY-SIX

"It happens. You get a big, strong horse and rider and a quick calf and sometimes the calf gets hurt," said Hal.

Jim brought his cup to the breakfast table and sat. "You all talking about yesterday?"

"Yes."

"You still upset about that?" Jim asked Sarah.

She nodded her head. "I'm not roping calves anymore."

"Rodeo's a tough sport," said Nell. "People get hurt all the time."

"She was a calf."

"Yes. But it could have been a person, or a bull, or a horse," said Nell.

"I'm not roping calves anymore."

Nell looked at Jim and then at Hal.

"No even the breakaways?"

Sarah shook her head.

"No one will make you."

"There's still barrel racing," said Hal. "You and Blackie against the clock."

Sarah nodded.

"And later, if you change your mind…"

"I won't."

"That's okay, too," said Nell.

TWENTY-SEVEN

Dean stood one foot up on the lowest rail of the fence surrounding the corral at the Gustafson ranch. He heard the kitchen door shut and turned to watch his father walk up to him carrying two mugs. Gus handed one to his son.

"Cream, no sugar," said Gus.

"Thanks, Dad."

Gus turned to the corral which was empty and put a foot up like Dean. The two stood for a couple of minutes before Gus said, "Maybe we could put a horse in there. You know, just so we were watching something besides an empty corral."

"You want me to get one of the guys?"

"Nah, they're all busy. You and I can do it. I'll get the door if you get the horses."

Gus balanced his mug on the fencepost nearest him and Dean did the same with another. Gus headed to the door with Dean following. Gus pulled one side open and Dean went in while Gus opened the other side. A moment later three horses trotted out into the corral followed by Dean. Gus and Dean closed the barn doors and went back for their coffees which were still steaming on the fence posts.

The horses' breaths were visible in the chill air.

"Dad, I'm sorry."

"For what?"

"I think I let you down."

"For not riding?"

"Yes."

Gus watched the horses move around the corral.

"That was probably the smart thing."

Dean looked at his father.

"A horse throws you and he immediately runs to the other side of the arena and tosses his head and kicks up his heels. It's like he's showing off or taking a bow for the crowd. He's so happy because he got rid of that scary rider on his back. 'Hey, look at me!' Gus waved his hand in the air. But when a bull throws you, he doesn't just want to be rid of you. You never know when he'll try to stomp you into dust so that you never come against him again. He's just as like to that as run away."

"And that's where the bullfighters come in?"

"Yeah, but that's not where I was going. Point is, there's a good reason to be scared of bulls. It might just mean you're smart."

"But you were a bull rider."

"Proves you're smarter than your old man."

"But now you're a bullfighter."

Gus smiled, "More proof."

"Why do you do it, then?"

"When I was your age, I did some rock climbing."

"You're afraid of heights."

"Yep. I was then, too. Never got over it. But I didn't want what I was afraid of to stop me from trying things. I didn't want fear to be the reason I didn't do something."

In the corral, the three horses chased each other around the ring.

The day didn't warm up much from the morning chill. The afternoon was still brisk and clear when Dean came round to Jim's ranch. Dean worked with Sarah while she rode Blackie around the barrels. Sarah stopped when she saw Dean.

"Go around a couple more times. Slow down a little – not all out," said Hal. Sarah clicked her tongue and she and Blackie went back at the barrels.

"You wanted to see me?" said Dean.

"Yeah, about yesterday."

They both watched Sarah circle the barrels. Blackie's muscles moved visibly under the sheen of his coat. Sarah leaned with him as he pounded round the barrels, first one way and then the next.

"I rode for years and there never was once when I didn't feel sick to my stomach before a ride." He looked at Dean. "Never a single time."

"Did you throw up, though?"

"More than I want to remember."

"You get over it?"

"I never did. There's tricks though that you can try that might help you."

"Tricks?"

"Yeah, some are mental, some physical. But not every trick works with every person. Sometimes it's hit or miss as to the effect so you try different ones to see which one works for you."

"You think you can help me?"

Sarah finished her run and rode Blackie to where Hal and Dean stood.

Hal opened the gate, "Bring him out."

Sarah rode Blackie out of the corral and slid out of the saddle. She handed the reins to Dean.

"Wait here," said Hal and he and Sarah went into the barn. Dean stroked Blackie on the forehead while he waited.

From the darkness in the barn, Dean saw Hal coming out holding a rope. Several feet behind Hal, he saw the bull on the other end of the rope. The rope was attached to the bull's nose ring. Sarah rode on Snodgrass' back. Dean could only stare as Hal walked the bull past him and made a slow circuit around the corral.

As they came full circle, the kitchen door slammed and Nell came running toward them. "Sarah," she called.

Hal stopped and the bull stopped with him. Nell stopped running and caught her breath. "Oh, my God. Hal, are you crazy?"

"No, ma'am. I don't think so."

Nell put both hands up in front of her and motioned downward. "Sarah, be careful," she said.

"I am, mom. It's okay."

"Hal, you get her off of there, right now."

Hal reached one hand up and helped Sarah down. He walked her around the front of Snodgrass and helped her climb over the fence.

"What were you thinking?"

Nell stared hard at Hal and then took Sarah by the elbow and walked her back into the kitchen.

Dean looped Blackie's reins around the rail and then walked back to his car and drove out of the driveway.

Hal watched them all walk away and then led Snodgrass back to the barn.

TWENTY-EIGHT

"What the hell was he thinking," said Gus as he turned the steaks on the grill behind his house. Dean stood next to him holding a bottle of beer.

"I don't know. He said he had something he wanted me to see."

"Sarah on the bull?"

"Yeah. But why he wanted me to see that, I don't know. Maybe he wanted me to see that I shouldn't be afraid. Maybe he was trying to show me up. I just don't get it."

"I don't get it either. Makes no sense at all. Here, you watch the steaks. I'm going to get some butter."

Gus turned the corner on the house and passed the table where four of his ranch hands sat and laughed. Gus was close enough to hear parts of the conversation as he walked.

"That Hal."

"He sure can ride," said Charlie.

"And he likes 'em young."

This brought more laughter from the group.

"Hal and his fillies," said Adam.

Gus turned and went over to the table where the hands got quiet.

"We too loud for you, boss?" said Hector.

"Nah, not at all. I just wondered what you were talking about."

"Nothing much," said Charlie.

"Aw, Charlie. I heard you men talking about Hal. Now what's this all about?"

The hands looked at one another and avoided Gus' eyes.

"Charlie?" said Gus. "Adam?"

"It's just talk, boss," said Paul.

"Okay." Gus stayed put and waited.

"We were in town at the bar and a pretty woman came in," said Charlie.

Gus looked around the faces at the table.

"And Adam...well it turns out it was Lizbeth."

"Lizbeth?"

"Lizbeth Arneson. Hal Comstock's ex."

"Ah, and Adam was hitting on her?" said Gus.

"Oh, come on, guys," said Adam.

"Well, you were," said Hector.

"And there was a confrontation between Hal and Roy Morris," said Charlie.

"Hal was there? And Roy Morris? The rodeo guy?"

"Yes."

"When did they show up?"

"Oh, they came in separately and sat next

to Lizbeth," said Paul.

"While Adam was hitting on her?" said Gus.

"Oh, Jeez," said Adam. "I was – I was back at the table already."

"Anyway, Hal and Morris sort of squared off and Lizbeth stopped it."

"While you guys sat around?"

All four men at the table exchanged glances.

"Yes," said Hector. "We didn't want to get in the middle of that."

"Probably a smart move," said Gus.

"After that, Hal left," said Charlie. "I tried to go after him. But before that, I heard Lizbeth say how Hal likes his women young."

"And maybe that's why he hangs around so much at Jim Rhodes' place," said Adam.

"Hmm," said Charlie. "Maybe that or the fact that he works there."

"We were just laughing, boss," said Paul. "We didn't mean anything by it."

Gus nodded and turned to finish his walk to the kitchen. He hoped the steaks weren't burnt.

TWENTY-NINE

Hal came in the back door at Jenet's after wiping his boots on the door mat. He wiped each boot twice. Jenet sat at her kitchen table. She worked at polishing a silver teapot that was part of a set. The tray, sugar bowl and creamer were as tarnished at the teapot and sat at the table across from her.

"That's a pretty set."

"My husband gave it to me. It was an anniversary gift. I don't use it much anymore." She rubbed at the teapot with a dish towel. "I should really wrap it in some silver cloth and store it away. But I like to look at it."

"Nothing wrong with that," said Hal as he watched her work. "I can polish if for you if you like."

"Not really what you would call ranching work."

"Still."

"Another time, maybe."

"All right. I'm all through outside. Everybody's fed and watered and the stables are all cleaned out."

"She's very pretty."

"Who?"

Jenet stopped polishing. "Lizbeth."

"Yeah."

Hal waited a moment before Jenet spoke again.

"Thank you, Hal. Friday?"

"Yes, ma'am. Friday."

Jenet went back to polishing the tea set as Hal went out the door.

THIRTY

"Is it fair to Hal?" said Gus as he ate supper with Abby. She had made his favorite: mushroom soup.

"Is it fair to Jim and Nell?" said Abby. "Or Sarah?"

"Hell, I don't know."

"And is it your call?"

"What do you mean?"

"If it were your daughter, wouldn't you want to know?"

"Yes. I would."

"Then, that's that."

Abby ladled some more soup into his bowl from the pot on the table.

THIRTY-ONE

Gus sat at a table in the only cafe in Bowman and stirred his cup of black coffee. The waitress named Carol had been by twice with the pot, but his cup was full both times.

Jim came into the cafe and spotted Gus and headed toward him. "A cup for me, too, please," he said to Carol as he passed her and took the seat opposite his friend. He reached across the table and shook Gus' hand.

"You eating?"

"Not hungry."

Carol put a cup on the table.

"We'll wait on ordering," said Jim.

"Sure thing," said Carol. "The menus are there when you need them."

Jim focused on Gus. "What's up?"

Gus stirred his coffee again and then put the spoon down on the still-folded napkin. The napkin absorbed what coffee remained on the spoon and it left a brown stain.

"I talked with Abby 'cause I wasn't sure."

"About?"

"About Hal. About whether or not to say

something."

"Hal?"

"Jim, you know I've didn't like him from the get go."

"Yeah, you didn't hide it."

"And you just sort of took him under your wing."

"Which you gave me grief for."

"Yeah."

Gus rocked his coffee first to one side and then the other.

"What is it, Gus?"

"Oh, hell." Gus took his hand off the cup. "I want to be fair to him."

"Gus?"

"Charlie and the boys went into town after the Roundup. They ran into Hal and his ex at the bar."

"I heard a little bit about that. The 'almost fight' between Hal and that cowboy, Roy Morris."

"Yeah, that."

Jim was watching Gus more closely now.

"From what I hear, there wasn't much to it."

"I'm talking about afterwards."

"Afterwards? I thought Hal left."

"He did. But before he left, the boys heard Lizbeth say some things I think you should hear."

Jim didn't stop him so Gus went on.

"I'd want to know."

Jim leaned forward and tilted his head to one side.

Gus picked up the spoon again and circled it once around the rim of his coffee cup. When he spoke again it was in a low voice so that only Jim could hear.

"Lizbeth said Hal likes young women."

Jim put his coffee cup to his mouth but didn't drink while he waited for more.

"Like -- Sarah-young."

Jim put his cup back on the table.

THIRTY-TWO

Jim knocked on the door to Hal's room above the barn. Nell said she'd seen him go up the stairs just after lunch. Jim heard movement on the other side of the door before it opened. Hal stood there with a toothbrush in his mouth. He motioned for Jim to come in while he rinsed his mouth in the small sink in the attached bathroom.

The room was neat except for the unmade bed. A few clothes lay about, but it did not make the room look cluttered. Still, Hal picked up clothes and put them into the bathroom.

"Boss?"

"Hal, I got to ask you a question."

"Shoot."

"Why did you break up with Lizbeth?"

Hal stopped moving. "What's this about?"

"Some of Gus' boys saw you with Lizbeth and Roy Morris at Rusty's in town last Saturday night after the rodeo."

"This about the fight?"

"No – maybe."

"'Cause we didn't actually come to blows.

Just words."

"Why did you and Lizbeth break up?"

"She left me."

"Why?"

"Why is this important, Jim? What difference does it make?"

"It's important."

Hal sat down on the bed. Jim remained standing.

"I had a habit of looking at other women."

"Young women?"

"Yeah."

"Keep going."

Hal spread his hands wide.

"At the shows, they'd parade the cowboys into the arena and all the buckle bunnies are standing on the rails waving and shouting and smiling at you. They rock back and forth and lean way over to give you a good look. Some of 'em wearing hardly anything beside a buckle, it seems. It's – well, it's distracting. It got to the point where I would walk in looking at the boots of the guy walking in front of me so I could keep my mind on the ride. Even then, it was still a distraction."

"Young women like Sarah?"

Hal looked up and then stood up.

"Like Sarah? Jim, you don't think..."

"I don't know what to think. That's why I'm asking."

Hal sat down again and looked at the floor.

"Sarah's like a daughter."

"Sarah is my daughter."

After a moment, Hal looked up.

"Jim, where did this come from? What made you ask me?"

"Does that matter?"

"Hell, yes."

Jim thought for a moment.

"Lizbeth said something to one of Gus' cowboys."

Hal put his head into his hands and sat still for a moment.

"What do you want me to do?"

"I want you to stay away from Sarah until I figure this out."

Hal sat motionless with his head still in his hands as Jim pulled the door closed behind him.

THIRTY-THREE

Sarah backed out of the kitchen door into the yard that afternoon after she got home from school. She no longer wore her backpack.

"Sarah," said Jim from inside.

Sarah looked toward the barn.

"Sarah, come back," said Nell as she came to the door.

Sarah backed away into the yard. "He's my friend," she said.

Jim stood at the door now, next to Nell. "Sarah, honey."

"He's my friend," said Sarah. "Nothing happened. How can you think that?"

Sarah turned and ran to the barn.

"Jim," said Nell.

Jim and Nell ran after her. Sarah reached the door to the stairs to Hal's room and opened it and ran up.

Jim and Nell reached the door to Hal's bedroom. Sarah stood inside. The room was clean, the closet empty and the bed made. Hal's rucksack was gone. The shaving kit Jim loaned him sat on the bed.

Nell moved forward and put her arm around Sarah's shoulders.

THIRTY-FOUR

Charlie came into Rusty's on Thursday night. The place was not crowded so he went straight to the bar.

"Coors, please."

"You drinking alone or will you join your friend?" said the bartender.

Charlie looked at him. The bartender put the bottle on the counter and motioned toward the far corner. Charlie turned to look. Hal sat there with his chair pushed as far back into the corner as it would go. He didn't look up even as Charlie pulled out the chair and sat down opposite him.

"You hiding out here?"

Hal looked up. It took a moment for him to recognize Charlie. He tilted his head sideways and shrugged.

"Mind if I sit?"

"You already are."

"Oh, yeah. Well, then you mind if I drink?"

Hal turned a palm up and motioned toward Charlie's bottle.

"You're very observant, tonight."

"It's my curse," said Hal. "At least it's one of them. One of many."

"What are you doing here, Hal?"

Hal looked at him for a moment before he said, "Same question."

"It's Thursday night. I wanted a beer after work."

"Me, too."

"I got my beer," Charlie said as he lifted his bottle. "What number are you on?"

Hal shook his head.

"How long since you stopped counting?"

"Who counts?" Hal raised a finger into the air, "Another one."

Charlie turned and waved the bartender off. Hal grabbed Charlie's wrist.

"What are you doing?" said Hal.

Charlie looked down at his wrist where Hal still held it. "You going to fight me too, Hal?"

Hal let go of Charlie's wrist and sat back in the chair. "Oh, that's right. You were here, too."

"Yeah," said Charlie. After a moment he added, "You haven't finished the one in front of you."

"Just trying to stay ahead of the curve."

Charlie watched Hal as he drank from his bottle and then took a long drink from his own. "Finish up. I'll get you home."

"No thanks," said Hal. "I got a ways to go, still."

THIRTY-FIVE

The light was different than Hal expected. The color was off or it was later in the day. He heard his own breathing first and then other breaths, deeper and longer than his own. He was lying on straw and had his boots on. He had slept all night with his boots on and his feet ached because of that.

He pulled himself up on the railing. He was in a stable or a barn. His hat lay in the straw a few feet away. He groaned as he reached for it and had to catch himself on the railing again or he would have fallen.

Even with the hat on his head, he had to shield his eyes from the morning sun. He heard the screen door bang against its frame. When his eyes adjusted to the light, he saw Jenet standing on her porch looking at him.

"Best come in, Hal."

Hal took a deep breath to steady himself and headed to the house. He took his hat off just before he walked through the door.

Inside, Jenet had already poured a mug of coffee and set it on the table. "Black, right?" she said.

Hal nodded and sat in the chair by the coffee.

"I remembered that because that's the name you came up with for Sarah's horse."

"Yes, ma'am."

Jenet watched Hal sip his coffee.

"Did Charlie bring me here?"

"Charlie? Haven't seen him."

"How'd I get here?"

"No idea."

Hal drank more of the coffee. Jenet folded her hands and rested her chin on them.

"How'd you know I was in the barn?"

Jenet smiled. "I heard you snoring."

"I snore?"

"You do. I came out to the porch when the snoring stopped. I figured you were either awake or dead. I took a chance and went with awake and waited for you to come out."

"I snore?"

Jenet laughed.

"Does Jim know I'm here?"

"I don't know. I didn't tell him. Should I?"

Hal shrugged.

"I expect he'll call you."

"And say what?"

"That I got into a fight – in a bar – with a cowboy – over Lizbeth."

"And did you?"

"Yeah, sort of. But we didn't really fight.

We just mouthed off at each other."

"Sounds like a hot time in town."

"Yeah."

"You still have feelings for her?"

Hal waited for a moment before answering. "I still get jealous at times, if that's what you're asking."

"Maybe. And what about Sarah?"

Hal looked up and put his mug on the table. "Sarah is my friend. And I was teaching her how to ride and do some rope tricks. And that's all."

Jenet waited for some moments before speaking. "Why would Lizbeth say what she said?"

"I don't know what she said. And I won't accuse her. But I'm being accused like I was making a play for Sarah."

"Jim is doing what he has to -- to protect his daughter."

"I know. And I know that I can't go back there."

Jenet picked up her cup and put it in the sink. "Well, you can still work your days here, if you want."

"You sure?"

She turned to face Hal. "I'm not afraid of Jim or Gus – or you."

Hal brought his mug to the sink and rinsed it. "No, ma'am. I don't think you're afraid of anyone."

He closed the screen door so it wouldn't

Eric Luthi

slam.

THIRTY-SIX

Dean stood with one leg up on the lower rail as Sarah rode around the barrels. Blackie's coat looked wet from the exercise. Dean could hear the horse's breaths as he leaned hard around the closest barrel. Sarah leaned so far with the horse she looked like she was about to fall off.

Dean checked the stopwatch.

"How fast," Sarah yelled back as Blackie slowed after the last turn.

"Eighteen five."

Sarah shook her head. "Again."

"You're a hard taskmaster," said Dean.

Sarah and Blackie came around and stopped at the railing

"I want to win. Blackie wants to win."

"You want to practice anything else? Throwing?"

"I don't – no, I don't think so."

"You were good at it."

Sarah shook her head.

Dean took a step closer to Sarah. He reached over the top rail and stroked Blackie on the forehead. "That was a special series of circumstances that caused that calf to die. The cowboy was big, the horse was big and they were both powerful. And that calf was small and fast. I've never seen that happen before. I never expect to see it again."

"But it could happen."

"You're not big enough. You and Blackie together don't have enough mass to stop a calf like that. It's a question of relative size and inertia."

"But it could happen."

"It could. But it's extremely unlikely."

Sarah said nothing.

"Okay," said Dean giving in. "Maybe you can try the ostrich racing in Fort Worth instead."

Sarah looked down at him from the horse.

"Why not? You get to ride in this chariot thing the ostrich pulls. You'll be like a gladiator."

Sarah narrowed her eyes.

"Just a thought," said Dean as he put his hands into the air. "Once more around the barrels."

Sarah moved Blackie to the starting point for their practice course.

"Go," said Dean as he pressed the stopwatch.

Sarah and Blackie raced around the barrels.

Sarah put Blackie in his stable and removed his saddle and bridle. She brushed him down.

"You did good today, Blackie. It was a good workout. Maybe we can get Dad to take us to practice at the Roundup on Wednesday. You keep going like today and you'll be a champion sure. And maybe you'll take me with you."

She finished brushing him and put a blanket over his back. The weather was cooling and he was still damp from the workout. She patted him one last time and went back outside to watch Dean.

Dean had Snodgrass in the corral. Jim came out to watch while Dean was with the bull. Dean had put one of the barrels in the corral as well. Snodgrass had no ropes on him anywhere. He was free to run around. Dean stood near the fence so he could jump out if needed.

"Can I ride him?" said Sarah.

"I don't think so, honey," said Jim.

"I rode him before."

"I'm not comfortable with you riding him or that I could keep you safe," said Dean.

Sarah frowned.

"Hal could do things with this bull that I wouldn't dare try," said Dean.

He watched the bull as he walked out into the middle where the barrel stood on its end. Snodgrass stayed to one end of the corral away from Dean. His eyes followed Dean but otherwise the bull didn't move. Dean held onto one side of the barrel's rim and moved it closer to the bull. Snodgrass eyed Dean and the barrel and then huffed and shifted his weight and turned sideways to Dean.

"Careful, Dean," said Jim. "He's presenting."

Dean nodded and walked the barrel forward by shifting its weight from side to side, moving an inch at a time.

Snodgrass huffed and dropped his head once and then twice.

Dean inched forward again. Snodgrass didn't move. Dean took a red handkerchief from his back pocket and flapped it open. Snodgrass twitched and huffed.

"Hah," said Dean as he waved the kerchief.

Snodgrass turned and charged with his head down. Sarah screamed. The bull's charge was so quick Dean didn't stay with the barrel but left it standing where it was and scrambled away. Snodgrass hit the barrel and knocked it across the corral. It bounced off the railing and rolled back into the center of the corral. Dean hopped on the fence and rolled over it to the outside where Jim caught him.

"Oh, boy," said Dean.

"You sure you want to do this? said Jim. "This?"

Dean looked at Sarah and then at Jim and broke into a huge grin. "Yeah."

Snodgrass stomped around the corral and hit the barrel again.

"Okay, then," said Jim. "I think we'll need some more wranglers."

Snodgrass hit the barrel once more.

THIRTY-SEVEN

It was a twenty-dollar fee to do a practice ride. Between the Bowman Roundup in October and the Fort Worth Rodeo in the bottom half of January, every Wednesday night was practice night in the Bowman arena. Next up were the bull riders. Hal took a seat in the stands. There was no fee just to watch.

A rider and bull came out of the gate. The bull was so-so but the rider was great. He lasted the full eight seconds. Not a prize-winning ride but respectable. Hal nodded his head and said, "Nice," under his breath.

The next two riders failed to make the eight second mark. They looked inexperienced but would improve with more practice.

Another rider made the qualifying time. With a better bull, he might be a prize winner. With a lesser bull, he'd have a tough time.

Dean stood on one side of the arena, watching the riders. He looked pale. Hal got up from his seat and went down to meet him.

Dean looked up when he heard his name.

"Hal. Where you been?"

"Around. Mostly working at Jenet Martin's. When do you ride?"

"I don't know. I paid the fee, but..." he patted his stomach. "I already threw up twice. They'll come back around to me again."

"How long?"

"Half hour or so. Maybe more."

"And then you'll ride?"

Dean forced a laugh. "Maybe," he said.

"Come with me," said Hal.

Hal turned and walked. Dean followed after a second. "Where are we going?"

"Snack bar."

"I couldn't..."

"Keep anything down?"

"No – yes."

"Don't worry. I don't have enough money to buy you anything."

The snack bar was not busy. Barely profitable on practice nights, the organizers opened it mostly as a courtesy to the riders and the few spectators who showed up to watch. Hal went up to the counter and spoke with the clerk. Dean couldn't hear what Hal said. Hal held up his thumb and forefinger showing an inch apart. The clerk nodded and stepped away. She returned a second later and handed a small gold-colored square to Hal. He closed his fist over it. Dean could see his mouth form the word, "Thanks."

"What was that about," Dean said when Hal got back to him.

"Let's go over here." Hal moved away from the snack bar.

"Okay, what?"

"Time to be Superman."

Hal smiled and opened his hand. On his palm, lay a single pat of butter in its foil paper wrapper.

"Butter?"

"Oldest trick in the book."

"Butter?"

"Sure cure for a nervous stomach."

"You gotta be kidding?"

"Never."

Dean took the pat of butter and held it up to the light. "What do I do with it?"

"Smear it on your face."

"No?"

"No. You eat it."

"Seriously?"

"You keep asking me that. Better eat it before it softens. Much easier to eat it while it's cold."

Dean peeled the foil paper off the butter while trying not to get his hands greasy. He dropped the paper and held the butter between his fingers.

"And this works?"

"Never fails."

Dean made a face as he bit down on the pat of butter and chewed. He swallowed hard and then worked his tongue around in his mouth to clear it.

"I'd rather eat peanut butter," said Dean.

"Who wouldn't?" said Hal.

The two walked back to the arena while Dean still worked his mouth.

"Where'd you learn about this?"

"I've heard about this for years."

"You're sure this works?"

"So I've heard."

Dean stopped.

"You've never tried this?"

"No."

Two steps later, Hal stopped and looked back. "How do you feel?" he said.

"Sick."

"See? Working already."

Hal and Dean stood outside the arena and watched the riders try out the bulls. Dean's pass had moved him to the end of the list once again. A rider and bull came out of the gate and the rider lasted only three seconds. He jumped clear and the bull went off in a different direction chased by the bullfighters.

"I'm sorry about the bull the other day," said Hal.

"The bull and Sarah?"

One of the two bullfighters in the arena sat

on the rail next to the chute. The only other bull-fighter stood at the other side away from Hal and Dean. Two girls wearing cowboy hats stood talking to the bullfighter on the other side.

"Yeah," said Hal. "I was trying to make a point and I don't think I made it so well. I didn't think it through."

A rider mounted a bull in the chute. The bullfighter jumped down from the rail and took his position in the middle of the arena in preparation for the ride. "George," he called to the bullfighter talking to the cowgirls. "George."

George glanced over his shoulder. "Be there in a sec, Walt." George screwed up his face and backed away from the girls toward the center. The cowgirls laughed.

"Don't worry about it," said Dean. "I think you made your point.

"Yeah? What point was that?" said Hal.

Hal and Dean both laughed.

The rider nodded. The latch man pulled and the gate swung open. The bull twisted out hard to the right and the rider lost his seat. The bull hit the ground hard with his front hooves and twisted right again and the rider was now loose. Only his hand still gripped the rope. Walt, the bullfighter in the middle of the arena, waved at the bull and moved in to assist. George, who had been talking to the cowgirls, now rushed to join.

The rider's hand and glove were pinched in the rope and he couldn't pull loose. The bull kicked and twisted and the rider flopped like a rag doll.

Dean jumped onto the fence and leaped over. Hal jumped onto the fence. In the arena, the bullfighter named Walt hung onto the bull and pulled hard at the rider's hand to free it while George tried to get into the mix from the other side but had a time trying to dodge the bull's horns.

"Hah! Hah!" yelled Dean as he waved his hat at the bull. The bull stopped spinning and kicking at Dean's approach. It sized up the new threat. Walt pulled the rider's hand loose leaving the glove still pinched in the rope. He dragged the unconscious rider back to the edge of the arena. George ran around behind the bull and helped pull the rider to the gate. The bull glanced at the three.

"Hah!" Dean shouted and stomped the ground. The bull looked back at Dean. A shiver started at its head and was visible as it ran back along the bull's spine all the way to his tail. The bull kicked its hind leg and pawed the ground with a front leg and snorted at Dean.

"Careful now, he's sizing you up," said Hal who now stood next to Dean.

The bull turned and glanced back at the bullfighters who now lifted the rider to the other hands that reached down from atop the gate to pull him out.

"Hah!" yelled Dean.

"Here we are," shouted Hal.

"Hoo, boy," shouted another wrangler who stepped up next to Hal. Another cowboy joined them on the other side of Dean.

The bull focused on the four and dropped his head.

"What now?" said Dean.

Hal spoke low. "Back up. Slow and together. If he charges, split up and run like hell."

The four cowboys backed away from the bull. The bull took one step toward them and then one more, matching the retreating cowboys step for step. He tossed his head and huffed. Then he dropped his head and charged.

"Go," shouted Hal. But he didn't need to say it.

The four turned and bolted for the fence, each one in a different direction away from the charging creature. The bull stopped, confused and unsure now of his target. Where there had been one, now he saw four. He looked first at one and then another of the fleeing enemies. By the time he focused on one, all four cowboys were up and over the fence and safe.

The few spectators and all the cowboys and riders and handlers and cowgirls stood and cheered and clapped. Hal's back got slapped more than a few times as he made his way over to

Dean who was surrounded so that Hal couldn't get close. Dean noticed Hal and touched the brim of his hat.

With his finger, Hal traced an "S" on his chest large enough so that Dean could see.

Dean grinned.

THIRTY-EIGHT

Jim had just leaned back in his chair and closed his eyes when he heard the truck come up the driveway. He didn't recognize the sound of the engine. The car door slammed and he heard his own kitchen door bang a second later.

"Jenet," said Nell.

A minute later, there was a soft knock at the door to his study. Nell opened the door and admitted Jenet.

"Whatcha working on?" said Jenet.

"My Sunday sermon."

"Caught you at a good time?"

"Actually, yeah. I'm sort of brain dead and need a break."

She sat in the chair opposite Jim. Jim waited for her to start the conversation since she had sought him out. After a few seconds, she did.

"I think you treated Hal unfairly."

"Oh?"

"I think you judged him too soon."

"I'm not sure I judged him at all."

"Then why isn't he still here?"

"How much do you know about what happened?"

"Most of it. You know there are no secrets in this town. What I didn't know, Hal told me."

"And what did Hal tell you?"

"That you accused him of pursuing Sarah."

"Well, not quite like that."

"But that's what you implied."

"That's what I asked. And then I asked him to stay away from Sarah until I could figure things out."

"And then?"

"And then he left."

"Jim, let me ask you, where did you hear this from?"

"From Gus."

"And he had it from?"

"Charlie."

"And Charlie got it where?"

"From Lizbeth."

"Hal's ex?"

"Yes."

"And this doesn't sound more than a little like that 'telephone' game we used to play as kids? A friend of a friend of a friend and the whole message gets distorted."

Jim sat for a moment before answering.

"I didn't ask him to leave. He left on his own."

"But you didn't ask him to stay, either."

"No."

"What else could he do? What would you

have done? You accused him of grooming your daughter. Maybe not with those words, but that's what you accused him of."

"I would have fought for my reputation."

"Well you're not Hal. You're Jim Rhodes. Not everyone can be a Jim Rhodes. Not everyone has a reputation to protect. Or one to rely on."

When Jim didn't answer, Jenet stood up. "You judged too soon."

She opened the door but turned back.

"When I hear one man's story, it sounds righteous. It sounds righteous." She made a fist. "Right up to the minute I hear the other man's side."

"Proverbs?" said Jim.

"Somewhere in there. Hal's been staying at my place. He works his days and leaves in the evenings. I hear he's been spending time at Rusty's. He sleeps in the barn and wakes up early, even when he's hung over."

Jim stood up but said nothing.

Halfway out the door, Jenet turned back to Jim. "I offered him the spare bedroom but he wouldn't take it."

THIRTY-NINE

Gus and Jim waited in the living room of Gus' ranch house when Charlie came in.

"You wanted to see me, Gus?"

"Yeah, Charlie. Actually, Jim did."

"Yes, sir."

"Have a seat, Charlie," said Gus. Charlie sat down.

"You know Hal doesn't work for me anymore?" said Jim.

"Yes, sir. I heard he was fired."

"Well – okay. You told Gus and Gus told me some things that were said about Hal."

"Uh."

"You're not in trouble, Charlie," said Gus. "But we want to know, as specifically as you can remember, the things that were said and who said them."

"Well, like you said the other day, Adam was hitting on Lizbeth in the bar that night. And then Hal came in. Adam retreated back to our table. We all gave him a time about that. A few minutes later that cowboy Morris joined them."

"Okay," said Gus. "But after that. After Hal

left."

"After Hal left, I went out after him."

"And that's when you heard Lizbeth talk about Hal?"

"No it was before that. While we were still at the table. The boys all heard it."

"So," Jim thought out loud. "Lizbeth said it while Hal was still there?"

"Yeah. In fact, it's probably what got Hal so upset. That's when he jumped up – when Morris laughed at that."

"What did you hear Lizbeth say?"

"She said, 'Hal likes his fillies.'"

"And that's all?"

"That's all I heard."

"What did you think she meant?"

"Adam thought she meant Hal liked his women young. He was joking about that when you came up that day, Gus, at the barbecue. He was saying about how that's the reason Hal spent so much time at your place, Mr. Rhodes."

Gus nodded and said, "What did you think she meant?"

"I thought they were talking about horses," said Charlie. "I mean – I assumed -- because they were both cowboys and all."

"And that made Hal upset?" said Gus.

"I think that wasn't until Morris laughed at him. At least it followed hard on that."

"What followed hard?"

"Hal jumped up and all."

"And that was after Morris laughed?"

"Yeah."

"Did Morris say anything before he laughed?"

"He was talking but I didn't hear what he said."

"About horses?"

"Yeah, could have been. At least with what Lizbeth said. It might have been about more – what's that word – when a word can mean more than one thing at the same time?"

"Double entendre?" said Jim.

'Yeah, that," said Charlie.

"What do you think?" said Jim after Charlie left them.

"I think there's less here than I originally thought. But I still would have come to you with it."

Jim nodded.

"And that still makes it your call."

FORTY

Jim found Hal in his corner at Rusty's, right where Charlie said he would find him. Hal said nothing as Jim sat down.

"Hello Hal."

Hal put a finger in the air to catch the bartender's attention. When the bartender looked over, Hal pointed down to his bottle.

"I'd order you one too, but..." said Hal.

Jim held two fingers in the air until the bartended nodded. A moment later, the bartender set two ice cold bottles on the table.

"I thought you didn't drink."

"I never said that. I said it was a dry ranch."

"My mistake."

"We all make them. Ain't a one of us perfect."

They sat for a few minutes. Jim sipped at his bottle. Hal didn't touch his.

"I'm sorry for what I said," said Jim. "I know I was wrong. I made assumptions I shouldn't have. I was wrong."

Hal played with his bottle but still didn't drink from it.

"You were," he said. "Wrong."

Jim leaned forward with his elbows on the table. "I hurt you and I'm sorry for it." He shifted in his chair and drew a circle on the table in the water dripping off his bottle. "I'd like you to come back to the ranch."

"What? And work for you again?"

"Yeah – if you'll forgive me."

"And that just fixes things? Just like that?"

"I hope so. Not sure what else I can do."

Hal sat back in his chair and tipped his bottle up and took a long drink.

When Jim left the bar, Hal still sat in his corner.

FORTY-ONE

It was mid-afternoon the following day when Jenet Martin's truck pulled into the Rhodes's driveway. The yard was quiet. All the horses and Snodgrass were in the stables or in the pastures. The truck door opened and Hal slid out of the driver's seat.

Sarah screamed from inside the house and flung the screen door open. She rushed down the stairs and collided with Hal midway across to the house. Nell came out the door a little less enthusiastically but she still smiled.

"Hal," screamed Sarah. "You're back."

"Well..." he paused. "Hello, Nell."

"Hello, Hal."

"You're back, right?" said Sarah. "You're staying?"

"I came back to say good-bye."

Sarah pulled back from him and looked at Nell and then back to Hal.

"I left too abruptly last time. I didn't get the chance."

"No, you can't leave. You have to teach me. Who'll teach me to ride and rope and catch calves?"

"Your father can. Or Dean. Or your mother. She used to be a champion. You'll do great, I know it. You don't need me."

She wrapped her arms around his waist and buried her face in his chest. "I want you to stay."

"I can't honey. It's better if I go. I have to."

He peeled Sarah's arms away from his waist. Nell came up and took Sarah and stepped back from Hal.

Hal looked at Nell. Sarah's face was turned away. Nell nodded and Hal turned back to his truck and climbed in.

Sarah looked up from her mother's side. "Why do you always have to take the hard path?"

Hal looked at her through the open window. Nell walked Sarah back to the house. At the door, Sarah pulled away from her mother. "You're a wild one," she shouted at Hal. "You're one of the wild ones. Why do you have to be wild?"

Hal waited until they were both in the house before he started the engine and drove away.

FORTY-TWO

It took Hal less than five minutes to put everything he owned into the rucksack. From inside the barn, he scanned the yard and the house. Nothing and no one moved. He slung the rucksack over one shoulder and walked to the gate and the road on the other side of it. On the road, he put his other arm through the rucksack's strap to that it rested on both shoulders and he headed west, away from town.

Jenet noticed the truck was back but didn't think more of it until that evening. At dinnertime, she went to the barn.

"Hal," she called.

The barn was empty. She went to the stall he slept in. It was empty, too, except for the straw he slept on. The blanket she'd given him was folded and hung across the railing.

She went back to the house and made dinner and ate alone.

That night, Hal slept in a field under a cloudy sky four hours walking distance from

Jenet's ranch. He groaned the next morning and walked crooked until the exercise warmed him up enough.

And then the rain came.

It wasn't a hard rain, but it was continuous. By the time he stopped at a stand of trees in the late afternoon, Hal was wet through. He dropped his rucksack at the base of a large bur oak and gathered up all the wood he could find. He even managed to find some dry twigs for tinder under another large tree.

The fire started small with just the twigs and some grass. Hal added more as the fire grew, moving on to the wetter branches which sizzled as the fire forced the moisture out of the wood. He piled on even more branches and moved closer to the fire and sat with his arms around his knees. The heat felt good and he closed his eyes.

He dreamt his feet were on fire.

The wet branches dried and caught and the fire had grown while he slept. Steam rose from the toes of his boots which were still on his feet. Hal pushed back from the fire and pulled his boots off and rubbed his toes through the socks which were still damp even though they were now hot. He set his boots upright by the fire to dry.

He piled the rest of his wood onto the fire and stood by it as it grew large again. At one point, the flames were as tall as he was. He looked up to watch the sparks rise high into the branches of the bur oak and disappear into the dark.

The fire died and Hal sat next to it again. He watched as the flames became embers and he lay down next to what was left and slept.

Hal spent all of the third day under the bur oak. His fire that night was a small one and that night, the sky was clear and Hal stayed awake to watch the stars.

In the afternoon of the fourth day after he left, Jenet looked out her window and saw Hal walking up her driveway. She went out to the front porch and waited. He stopped at the foot of the stairs.

"You look lost, cowboy."

Hal looked at the barn and then back to Jenet.

"I don't know whether I'm coming or going."

"Well, I haven't seen you in a few days. And you look to me like you're arriving. So, based on the evidence in front of me, I'd say you're coming."

"Yes, ma'am." Hal smiled and nodded toward the barn. "Is my spot still open?"

"And the bedroom inside, too."

Hal nodded.

"Dinner's at six," said Jenet.

FORTY-THREE

Jenet carried the groceries from the truck into the kitchen. She had left early on a trip to town. She'd heard Hal poking about the barn but didn't want to disturb him. He always found enough work to keep himself busy on the days he worked for her. He hadn't sought her out that morning and she didn't push him.

Now it was quiet. She came out onto the porch and listened. No sound came from the barn. She went back inside and walked through the house.

Something about the living room was odd. Jenet noticed it the moment she stepped through the door. The light in the room was different. She stepped back into the hallway and then reentered the room to make sure. It just looked different. She walked across the room and saw it when she turned around.

The tea set was still in the glass-front cabinet where it always sat. But instead of blending in with the background, instead of just being there, it was bright, polished to a high shine. Jenet opened the door and took out the teapot. It hadn't been this shiny since it was brand new, the day her husband gave it to her fresh out of the box on one of their first anniversaries. She rubbed the surface with her thumb and then took out the sugar spoon. She could see her reflection in the bowl of the spoon. The distortion of her face made her smile.

And then she cried.

FORTY-FOUR

Dean held the stopwatch high as Sarah and Blackie raced towards him after turning the last barrel. Gus and Jim stood next to him as Dean pressed the button with his thumb just as horse and rider crossed the finish. Sarah and Blackie slowed in a big loop around all three barrels as Sarah looked back.

Dean looked at the stopwatch, "Fifteen flat."

Sarah brought Blackie up to the starting point and waited.

"Go," yelled Dean and pressed the start button on the stopwatch.

Sarah yelled, "Hah." Blackie raced forward. Sarah didn't need to remind him with her heels. Her voice was enough to start him racing.

Blackie charged toward the first barrel to the right of the starting position and he and Sarah leaned in hard for the right turn. They shot across in front of the men watching toward the inside of the second barrel and made a hard left turn, leaning all the way around and came out of the turn facing the third barrel at the northern end of the course. Blackie pounded the turf loose and his hooves tossed clumps of dirt into the air behind him as he charged for the last barrel. He and Sarah aimed for the right of the barrel and made another hard left turn. Blackie's hooves dug deep as he arrested his momentum and ripped around the last barrel.

They came out of the turn facing south and a straight shot toward the finish where Gus and Jim and Dean waited. Dean held the stopwatch high once more.

"Go, Sarah."

"C'mon. Push."

Blackie raced past the men as Sarah's ponytail streamed behind her.

Dean looked at the stopwatch. "Fourteen point seven. Fastest time ever."

Sarah let Blackie cantor to a walk and then brought him around to where the men waited. Jim patted her on her leg. Dean took hold of the bridle.

"I think I sold him too cheap," said Gus. "Want to sell him back to me?"

"No," said Sarah. "Not ever."

"Nice try," said Jim.

They all laughed.

Sarah looked down the driveway toward the road. Hal walked into the driveway with his rucksack across one shoulder. Sarah threw one leg over the saddle horn and slid to the ground. She ran to Hal who was halfway up the driveway but stopped a few feet shy of him.

"I'm sorry," said Hal.

Sarah rushed forward and hugged him as Jim and Gus and Dean came up.

"Are you staying?" said Sarah.

"I'd like to," said Hal as he looked to Jim. "On the days Jenet can spare me."

"Of course," said Jim.

"Yay," said Sarah.

"Oh," said Hal and put his rucksack on the ground and opened the top. He dug down deep into it and came up with one of his spurs. The tarnish gone, it was polished to a white shine and the leather strap cleaned and oiled and looking like new. He stood and held the spur out to Dean.

"Your turn," said Hal.

Dean took the spur and rubbed his thumb over the surface.

"You got to use 'em to keep 'em shiny," said Hal.

Dean looked up from the spur to Hal, "I will if you will."

Hal said nothing.

"Hey," said Sarah. "What about me?"

Hal reached down into his rucksack and pulled out the spur's mate, also polished and looking new.

"The funny thing about spurs is that they always come in pairs."

He handed the spur to Sarah.

Sarah looked from the spur to Dean. Dean nodded to her and Sarah looked back to Hal. "I will if you will," she said.

Hal looked at the faces around him.

"Guess I don't have a choice."

FORTY-FIVE

Even though these were only the preliminary events, the stadium at the Fort Worth Stock Show and Rodeo was full to capacity. In the concession area, a man bought hot dogs and sodas for his children and carried the goods back to the stands where they waited. A little girl nearby kept her hands warm with her cup of hot chocolate rather than drink it on this cold January evening.

Rodeo clowns romped in the arena as the riders and contestants prepared themselves backstage. The breakaways would be first. Sarah's event.

The first five riders performed without mishap. All were older than Sarah and all performed with respectable times.

"Next up, Sarah Rhodes on Black Works," said the announcer.

In the stands, Nell and Jim Rhodes and Abby Gustafson sat behind the front row railing, Nell took her husband's hand. Jim gripped back as Sarah rode Blackie to the back of the box and turned him around to face the opening.

Jenet Martin came up a little out of breath

and sat down next to Nell. "Just in time. I heard them call her name. I didn't want to miss this."

"Yeah, she's up next," said Abby.

"Look," said Jim pointing. The whiteness of her spur stood out against the horse's black coat.

"Maybe she'll have a matching set one day," said Jenet.

In the arena, the calf watched the crowd and Sarah watched the calf. She saw her parents in the stands but was too nervous to wave. She nodded to the latch man. He swung the gate open and the latch man shouted, "Hah."

The calf ran out of the chute.

Sarah counted, "One, two."

Blackie stamped the ground as the calf ran away. Sarah had to hold him back.

On three Sarah shouted, "Go, Blackie, go." The horse charged forward so fast Sarah had trouble staying in the saddle. She recovered and swung the rope around her head as they passed the barrier and the clock started counting.

Blackie didn't so much chase the calf as cut diagonally across the arena to where the calf would be in another second. Sarah swung rope hard and launched it. As the noose flew over Blackie's head, he dug his hooves into the turf and Sarah leaned back in the saddle. The calf still ran as the noose dropped over its head. The rope tightened and the white flag tore loose from Blackie's saddle horn and the clock stopped. The calf continued to run around the arena now trailing the rope with the white flag on the end.

The handlers removed the rope and herded the calf back into the pen where it would wait for another turn.

Sarah and Blackie waited in the center of the arena.

"Six point three seconds," said the announcer.

Sarah leaned forward and patted Blackie on the neck.

One of the bullfighters in clown makeup came over to their side of the arena and jumped up to grab the railing in front of Abby. His face looked funny with his makeup smile at a crazy angle on both sides of his mouth.

"You going for the Joker there, Gus?" said Jenet.

"Or maybe it's a little bit John Wayne Gacy?" said Jim.

Nell slapped his hand.

Gus laughed. "Pure unadulterated Gus Gustafson." He leaned forward to Abby. She took his face in her hands and kissed him. He leaned more and rubbed his cheek against hers leaving a smudge.

"Gus, you're getting your makeup all over me."

"It's only fair."

"Gustafson, you're terrible," said Abby.

Gus jumped down from the railing. "Gotta

go," he said and ran off.

"A clown's work is never done," said Abby.

Gus turned and ran backward. "A bull-fighter's work."

"Yes, dear."

Two hours later was the bull riders turn. The contestants and made their walk into the arena. The crowd stood and cheered. The walk-way fence was lined with fans, many of them young women, shouting and trying to catch the riders' attention.

"There's Dean," said Sarah. She wore the white ribbon she received for placing fourth in the breakaway competition.

Dean came in near the end of the parade. Hal walked behind him. Behind Hal walked Roy Morris.

"Are we going to see fireworks?" asked Nell.

"God, I hope so," said Abby.

"You drew first ride," said Hal.

"Yeah," said Dean.

"Good. Get it over with quick. Before you have time to get sick."

"No chance of that." Dean took a folded foil wrapper from his shirt pocket and showed Hal.

"Well, then, Superman. How can you lose?"

"Yeah." Dean tucked the wrapper back into this shirt pocket. "I'd better go."

Dean fastened his helmet as he walked toward the chute. Roy Morris, who had been wait-ing, now came over to Hal and held out his hand.

"I wanted to apologize."

"For?"

"For the other day in the bar. I was – I was just being stupid."

Hal took his hand. "No harm done. Is Liz-beth here?"

"She's in the stands. She wanted to hold back and say hello later."

Hal nodded.

"You're a good man, Comstock. Good luck with your ride today."

"And you, Morris."

Hal walked to the fence and climbed up to watch Dean's ride.

Dean stood on the railing and patted the bull to let him know he was there. The bull was Clancy, a new bull without a reputation one way or the other. The handler checked Dean's vest and helmet and helped him fasten his rope around the bull. Dean climbed over the top rail.

"You okay," said the handler.

Dean nodded.

"First ride?"

"Yep."

"Okay. He's facing to the left, so his first turn, when the gate opens, is going to be to the right -- into the arena."

Dean nodded again.

"Make it past that and the rest is up to you."

Dean eased his right leg over Clancy's back but kept his weight on his left leg which remained on the rail. The bull huffed but didn't move. Dean lowered his weight onto the bull's back and cinched the rope tight.

"Whenever you're ready, cowboy."

He looked to the latch man and nodded.

The handler stood up on the rail.

The latch man swung the gate open.

Clancy sat still for a brief moment. Dean didn't wait but touched his spur to the bull's left side.

Hal's spur.

Clancy didn't need to be reminded twice. At the touch of the spur he broke hard to the right and kicked his back legs up. Dean hung on with his left hand and waved his right hand to try to balance against the bull's moves. Mostly, his hand just flopped around in the air as Dean tried to keep it from touching the bull.

Clancy spun to the right three times while kicking with his hind legs. When that didn't work to dislodge the rider, Clancy ducked his head low and spun to the left. The change in direction caused Dean to lose his grip with his knees but he pulled up hard with his rope hand and got his butt back down to the bull's back.

Eight seconds is a long time when you're engaged with a bull in a ring. Dean's only focus had been to hang on so the buzzer surprised him when

Eric Luthi

it sounded. With his peripheral vision, he could see the bullfighters moving in. On Clancy's next buck, Dean threw his right leg across the bull's back and dropped to the ground. He rolled on the impact and got to his feet with the help of one of the bullfighters who hustled him to the fence.

In the stands Nell and Jim and Sarah and Abby and Jenet Marting were all on their feet.

The crowd cheered.

Abby cried.

In the arena, one of the bullfighters pounded both fists into the air several times. His smile, crazy and smudged before, was even more smudged and smeared now.

And his cheer was the loudest.

Dean found Hal on a bale behind the riders' lounge. He wasn't inside with the other riders so Dean figured to check outside.

Hal stood up and shook Dean's hand.

Dean turned it into a hug.

"You did good," said Hal.

"I won't win any ribbons. I barely held on."

"Are you kidding me? You held on for eight seconds. Not everyone can say that. That's a win right there."

Dean held out the spur. "You want this back? For luck?"

"Nah. That's yours now."

"Okay," said Dean. "But you're almost on deck. What are you doing out here?"

"Getting ready."

"And are you?"

"Sort of."

"You'll do well."

"Says the man whose ride's already behind him."

"As yours will be, soon. What bull did you draw?"

"Wodan."

"Oh."

"Yeah."

"Well..."

Hal shrugged. "Wish me luck."

"Luck. Oh, I think you forgot something," said Dean.

Dean dug into his shirt pocket and pulled out a small square wrapped in foil. He held it out to Hal.

"Your turn."

Hal smiled and took the pat of butter. "It's soft."

"Well, I've been carrying it around looking for you."

"It's supposed to be cold. Didn't I teach you anything?"

"I did the best I could."

Hal tried to peel the wrapper but his fingers kept slipping. In the end, he managed one corner. He squeezed from the closed end, flattening it as if it were a tube of toothpaste and forcing the soft butter out of the open corner and into his mouth.

He made a face as he sucked the last of the butter from the paper and swallowed it.

"Ugh."

"How do you feel, now?"

"Sick."

Dean laughed.

"See, working already."

Hal climbed onto the railing. His bull, like Dean's, faced left. But this bull wasn't as quiet. He snorted and butted and crashed against the metal railings loud enough for the crowd in the stands to hear the ruckus.

The loudspeaker crackled. "A record crowd here tonight and we have a special treat for you all. Tonight, two-time all-around champion, Gene Henry Comstock, returns to the rodeo world for the first time in fourteen years."

The crowd cheered and the bull crashed into the gates again.

"Gene Henry will ride 'Vo-dan.'" The announcer dragged the name out, emphasizing the German pronunciation.

The crowd roared and then hushed to a silence as all eyes watched Hal climb inside the stall and stand above the restless bull. The bull hit the fence again. Hal waited for the animal to settle down.

"Looks like Wodan is giving Gene Henry a tough time already," said the announcer.

The wrangler and the latch man both

watched Hal's face.

"How's it going, Gene?" said the wrangler.

"I'll tell you in eight seconds."

"I bet you will."

Gus, still in his bullfighter's garb, came up behind the latch man and put his hand on the gate. "I got this," he said.

The latch man looked up at Hal. Hal nodded.

Hal still stood over the bull straddling both sides of the chute. He ran his hand down Wodan's back and felt him tremble. The bull crashed against the gate again.

Hal looked up at Gus.

"I appreciate what you did for Dean," said Gus.

"It was just butter."

"You and I both know it was more than that."

The bull snorted and stamped its feet.

Hal looked at Gus a moment longer and then lowered himself until the bull held his full weight. He gripped the rope tight with his left hand and held onto the railing with his right.

"You ready?" said the wrangler. He looked directly into Hal's face, waiting for the signal.

Hal nodded to Gus and fixed his eyes on the bull's neck.

Gus pulled on the latch.

"Ride 'em, cowboy."

The gate swung open and bull and rider

stormed out into the arena.

- THE END -

CPSIA information can be obtained
at www.ICGtesting.com
Printed in the USA
LVHW011508281019
635545LV00002B/477